Be First in the Universe

Be First in the Universe

Stephanie Spinner
and
Terry Bisson

DELACORTE PRESS

Published by
Delacorte Press
an imprint of
Random House Children's Books
a division of Random House, Inc.
1540 Broadway
New York, New York 10036

Visit us on the Web! www.randomhouse.com/kids
Educators and librarians, for a variety of teaching tools, visit us at
www.randomhouse.com/teachers

Library of Congress Cataloging-in-Publication Data

Spinner, Stephanie.
 Be first in the universe / Stephanie Spinner and Terry Bisson.
  p. cm.
 Summary: While staying with their hippie grandparents, ten-year-old twins, Tod
and Tessa, discover an unusual shop at the nearby mall, where they find a lie-
detecting electronic pet, a Do-Right machine, and other alien gadgets which help
them foil their nemeses, the evil Gneiss twins.
 ISBN 0-385-32687-4
 [1. Twins Fiction. 2. Extraterrestrial beings Fiction. 3. Science fiction.]
I. Bisson, Terry. II. Title.
PZ7.S7567Be   2000
[Fic]—dc21   99-39933
                                                                    CIP

The text of this book is set in 13-point Goudy.
Book design by Debora Smith
Manufactured in the United States of America
February 2000
10 9 8 7 6 5 4 3 2 1

For aliens everywhere
—S.S. and T.B.

chapter 1

They were twins, but they weren't really alike, not in Tessa's opinion. Tessa had lots of opinions, and she expressed them freely. Her brother, Tod, kept his opinions to himself. But Tessa knew him so well that she could usually tell what he was thinking, even if he didn't say a word. Right now, for example, she knew exactly what was on his mind.

A propeller.

A broken propeller.

"Earth to Tod, Earth to Tod," she said in a nasal robot voice, waiting for him to put down his pliers. It was as if he were in a trance, she thought. He was sitting in one of his favorite places, at the old Formica table under the locust tree in their grandparents' big, overgrown front yard, but he could have been in outer space.

It was always like that when he fooled around with something broken. Give Tod an old radio, a rusty windup toy, or a broken propeller like the one for his science fair project, and he got all quiet and intent until he fixed it, which could take all day.

Tessa didn't have all day. She stood over him, willing him to pay attention.

"What?" he asked, not even looking up.

"We're going!"

"Where?" It was hardly a question. His attention was on the propeller shaft, which was bent. He straightened it slowly and methodically, the way he did most things.

"Guess!"

Tod flicked the propeller and it began to turn. "Aha," he murmured, pleased. He finally looked up at her. "I give," he said.

"The mall." She grinned.

"Really?" His dark eyebrows shot up.

"Yes!"

Middle Valley Mall was the newest and biggest mall in the state. The twins liked malls a lot—when they were living at home with their parents, they went to them all the time. They even had a list of favorites, which they ranked according to Best Fast Food, Best Escalators, and Best Bathrooms.

But this year they hadn't been to a single mall, because they were living with their grandparents while their parents traveled through the Far East on business.

The twins loved staying with their grandparents. Lou and Lulu were relaxed and funny, and their ranch was a great place. It had a pond and fields and a barn with an old jukebox in it that Lou played when he milked his goats. And because it was close enough to their "real" home, the twins didn't have to change schools.

However, there were some drawbacks to living with Lou and Lulu. The twins had to do chores. They had to give up a lot of their favorite television shows because the ranch didn't have cable. And they had to deal with Lou and Lulu's only real failing—their dislike of malls. They didn't think kids should hang out in them, or even visit them.

Lots of kids at school had already been to the brand-new mall. Tessa's friend Lisa said it was vast, that you practically needed hiking shoes and trail mix to get through it. Tod's friend Spike got a free glow-in-the-dark yo-yo the day he went.

Tessa started complaining to Lulu that she had a rare disease called mall deprivation. Depression and bad moods and nail-biting were its main symptoms, she said. But this strategy didn't work. Every time she or Tod asked if they could go, Lou and Lulu came up with a reason why they couldn't. The mall was too big. Too confusing. Too expensive.

"At least they can't say it's too far," Tod had said to Tessa after their last attempt.

"A mile." Tessa had sighed dramatically. "Just one itty-bitty bike ride from here. You know," she'd added, "they never actually said they *forbid* us to go."

"They're the world's oldest living hippies," said Tod, who was very matter-of-fact. "They don't use words like *forbid.*"

Their grandparents, who insisted on being called by their first names, had gone to Woodstock, traveled to India, and then moved to a commune in Vermont, where Lulu wrote and illustrated a book of organic vegetarian recipes that became a bestseller and kept selling year after year. Now, thanks to *The Cosmic Kitchen*, they raised goats and organic vegetables on their farm, the Double L Goat Ranch.

Lou and Lulu didn't even use credit cards, much less go to malls. When they had to buy anything they went to small stores run by people they knew.

"So how come they gave in?" asked Tod now, as he and Tessa jumped on their bikes. This was another way she and Tod were different, thought Tessa. She could never wait five whole minutes, the way Tod had, to ask why their grandparents had finally changed their minds about something so vitally important.

"It was Lulu, actually," said Tessa as they pushed off. "She got a rush order for bread pudding and it turns out she doesn't have enough pans, and Trudy's is closed." Trudy's was the little general store where Lulu shopped—or bartered.

"So we have to find them at the mall. 'Large, rectangular, nonstick ones,'" she recited, imitating Lulu's soft Southern accent.

The twins' grandmother was a wonderful cook who specialized in baked desserts made with home-grown, organic ingredients. The local people had always bought her muffins and fruit pies; Trudy had started selling them when Lou and Lulu bought the ranch. But a few years earlier some fancy stores in Philadelphia and New York had begun to sell them too. Now Lulu had standing orders for Piece of My Heart Chocolate Cake and Wild Thing Cannoli, her two most popular confections.

There were also people who called the ranch and ordered directly. Lulu didn't advertise or have a Web site (their computer was so old it had a black screen and orange letters), but every now and then some health-conscious person with a sweet tooth managed to track her down. They were the ones who loved her desserts so much that they got completely emotional about them, like the woman who'd called today.

"Lulu may hate malls," said Tessa, pedaling hard to keep up with Tod, "but she's a complete pushover for a customer in tears."

"The woman cried?" Tod looked shocked. Tessa rolled her eyes at his reaction. He was always surprised when people got worked up about things. Their mother was like that too—calm and businesslike. Tessa was more like their father. She liked excitement. And she was anything but quiet.

"Yes! And Lulu caved right away! Is that luck or what? Thank you, Mrs. Crybaby!" Tessa yelled, standing up on her pedals. The back road was curvy but it was flat, and they were really whizzing along.

Suddenly Tod screeched to a halt. Tessa circled around and pulled up next to him.

He pointed.

Below them lay a vast parking lot, filled with hundreds, maybe thousands of cars. It was full of people, too—carrying packages, pushing strollers, streaming into the building at the far end of the lot.

The building, sky blue and painted with fluffy white clouds, was topped by a pulsing neon rainbow. Exploding neon stars, like fireworks, flashed and glittered over the entrance with its gigantic MIDDLE VALLEY MALL sign. Deep, twangy music came their way on the breeze. It was harp music.

"Yow. This is bigger than the Beverly Center," said Tessa, referring to a shopping center in Los Angeles that was so big it was almost like a city in itself.

"It might even be bigger than Danbury," said Tod. The Danbury mall in Connecticut *was* as big as a city. And its Sears had the largest tool department on the East Coast, which made that mall Tod's personal favorite.

They stood there for a moment, admiring the Middle Valley Mall in reverent silence. Then Tod got back on his bike. "On your mark," he said, getting ready.

"Set." Tessa crouched over her handlebars.

"Go!" They were off.

chapter 2

A few minutes later they'd locked up their bikes and were part of the throng hurrying through the rows of revolving doors. Once they were inside the brightly lit multilevel arcade, they quickly found the mall directory, a large sign that listed dozens of stores—from Aladdin's Cave of Carpets to Mighty Tights to Weird Houseplants of the World.

Though the harp music was softer than the roar of hundreds of shoppers on the move, the twins could hear it plinking every now and then as they looked for the name of a store that would have cooking supplies. The tune sounded familiar to Tessa, like one of the bouncy old songs from the sixties on Lou's jukebox.

Tod pointed to one of the directory listings. "How about this one?" he asked. "Gourmet Gallery."

"Sure." Tessa saw that it was on Level 3. "Escalator!" she exclaimed, leading the way. She loved escalators, which were so much better than elevators, in her opinion, because you could look around while you were on them. Rising to Level 2, for example, they saw a mother pushing a stroller with triplets in it, somebody wearing a rooster costume, a man dressed in angel's robes handing out popcorn, and two girls wearing grass dresses and flowerpot hats.

"They must be from Weird Houseplants of the World," said Tessa. She could tell that Tod was enjoying the spectacle just as much as she was. His eyes were wide and his jaw had dropped an inch, which was his way of saying "Whoopee."

Another minute and they were on Level 3, which looked just like Levels 1 and 2, except for the stars in the blue domed ceiling that flashed in time to the music.

"Right or left?" asked Tessa as they stepped off the escalator. They could always find each other if they split up—it was an odd gift they had—but she'd promised Lulu that she and Tod would stick together at the mall.

"Left," said Tod. They turned in unison and made their way past stores full of women's clothing, music, coffee and tea, bath stuff, and cosmetics. Then they walked up the other side past candles, toys, and men's shoes until they reached Gourmet Gallery.

It was a big, high-ceilinged store whose shelves were lined with brightly packaged food—Swiss chocolate, French fruit syrups, Swedish crackers, English jams and jellies, and Italian, Greek, and Spanish olive oil. Salamis and cheeses in ropes hung over the counter. Long breads were piled up in baskets, and hills of olives—big, small, wrinkled, smooth, and stuffed—filled the display cases. Everything looked foreign and expensive. Even so, the shop was full of people.

There wasn't a pan in sight.

"Where to now?" asked Tessa. "There has to be a cooking shop here somewhere."

"Maybe not," said Tod. They stood there for a moment as shoppers swirled by. Tessa could tell that her brother was thinking about something else. Probably his propeller.

"Head home?" he asked.

"I know you want to work on that project thing—"

"Wind generator," said Tod. "For the science fair."

"—but we can't leave Lulu stranded," Tessa finished.

"We didn't notice any other kitchen stores, re-member?" Tod started walking to the escalator.

"Wait! Let me think." Tessa grabbed his hand and started walking backward, which she liked to do when she was figuring something out. She claimed it helped her to concentrate.

Against his will, Tod fell into step with her.

It was on their second step in unison that it hap-pened.

chapter 3

*T*od saw a flash of red, so fleeting it could have been imaginary. But his imagination never played tricks with him, he thought, taking another backward step. Tessa was the one who got carried away with that stuff.

He took another step and it happened again. A flash of light, bright red, in the corner of his eye.

"Did you see that?" he asked Tessa.

"What?"

"That." He pointed. Reflected in the window of Home Office Depot was a sign:

GEMINI JACK'S U RENT ALL

It blinked on, then off.

It blinked on again. The twins saw that underneath, in smaller letters, there was more:

Be First in the Universe!

"There's something weird about that reflection," said Tessa.

"You're right. Reflections should be backwards," said Tod. "That one isn't."

The reflection disappeared.

"Where's it coming from?" Tessa peered around. "Where'd it go?"

"Hard to figure," murmured Tod. "Hmmm. Let's try something," he said, taking his sister's hand. As soon as they started to walk backward again, it appeared:

GEMINI JACK'S U RENT ALL
Be First in the Universe!

It blinked on, then off.

Tod looked to the right. Tessa looked to the left. "There," she said, pointing. A red neon sign glowed at the end of a narrow corridor they hadn't seen before.

"Let's check it out," said Tessa, who loved mysteries.

"You think we'll find pans?" said Tod, who loved solutions.

Tessa didn't answer. She was halfway down the corridor, so Tod chased after her. The concrete floor was dusty with the white dust of construction, as if it were new. Or newer than new—the corridor seemed like a part of the mall that hadn't opened yet.

The sign was flickering over a glass door at the end of the corridor.

"It's like it's blinking in and out of existence," said Tod. He paused to watch it disappear again. Tessa was thinking they should hurry. Lulu expected them back with the pans.

The twins walked through the door and heard a *Bong!*

"Cool," said Tod. It was like walking into a video game. Inside, a white counter faced the door. A sign on the counter said ONE FREE FOR TWO SALE. There were no shelves, no displays, no stacks of merchandise, no cash register, no customers, and no salespeople.

Tod blinked. A short, thin man wearing a silvery jumpsuit appeared behind the counter. At first Tod thought he was a workman. But the man smiled and said, "What can I do for you?" So he wasn't a workman.

"Do you carry cooking supplies?" asked Tessa.

"Like nonstick baking pans?" asked the man, reaching under the counter. He pulled out a shopping bag that said the same thing as the sign:

GEMINI JACK'S U RENT ALL
Be First in the Universe!

Tessa peered into the bag. There, nestled together at the bottom, were three baking pans. "How did you know what we wanted?" she asked.

"Lucky guess," replied the man. Tessa was wondering why his face had no wrinkles as he added, "We rent those, too."

"What?" asked Tod.

"Lucky guessers," said the man. "Handy little items." He smiled again, his very dark eyes fixed on them.

He doesn't blink, thought Tessa. And his skin . . . it's perfect. No lines. No wrinkles. A tiny chill snaked up her back.

"Gemini Jack's is the place to visit for all your needs," the man went on. "Why buy when you can rent?"

"Makes sense," said Tod. He couldn't take his eyes off the man's face. It seemed impossible, but the man's mouth appeared when he was talking and disappeared when he wasn't. Tod's eyes slid over to Tessa. She was staring at the man with her mouth open.

"You kids just call me Jack."

"Well, uh, Jack," said Tod, "we need three non-stick baking pans and we'd like to ah, rent them for a day."

"Consider it done," said Jack, entering some figures into a handheld computer that appeared in his palm. He seemed to have too many fingers. But when Tod tried to count them, he couldn't—they moved too fast.

"These pans—are they really nonstick?" asked Tessa, who was a careful shopper.

"Guaranteed one hundred percent friction free," said Jack.

"How much?" asked Tod.

"A one-day rental is two dollars," said Jack. He entered more figures into his palmtop. "That's per pan. So the total would be . . ."

"Six dollars," said Tod. He reached into his pocket for the fifty-dollar bill Lulu had given him, unfolded it, and laid it on the counter. "Out of fifty," he said.

Jack was already shaking his head. "Plastic only," he said. "I'm not set up for paper."

"Plastic?" said Tod. "We're kids. We don't have credit cards."

"Our grandparents don't believe in them," said Tessa.

"How unusual," said Jack. His dark eyes glittered. "How can they not believe in something that is all around them?"

"They were at Woodstock," said Tod. "They have different values. They try to live off the land, without harming anything. You know. Hippies."

Jack's face didn't move, though his eyes watched them carefully. Tessa wondered if he understood what Tod was talking about. "They barely believe in money," she said. "If they had their way, everything would be barter."

Jack's eyes brightened. "Barter is good," he said. "It's used in lots of worl—I mean malls. What do they barter?"

"Vegetables," said Tod. "Goat's milk."

"Pies and cakes," added Tessa. "Herbs. Tie-dyed pot holders."

"I see," said Jack. His smooth forehead wrinkled for an instant. "However, I have no need for any of those items."

"What's the one-free-for-two sale?" asked Tessa. "Don't you mean a two-for-one sale?"

Jack shook his head. "One free for two," he said. "One free rental for twins."

"Really?" cried Tessa. "That's us! We're twins!"

Jack's black eyes flashed and his face somehow got brighter, as if it were lighting up from inside. He stared at Tessa, then at Tod. "Are you really twins?" he asked with a new intensity in his voice. "You don't look one hundred percent alike."

"Absolutely," said Tessa, who knew better than anybody how different she and Tod really were. It wasn't just that her hair was red and curly and his was brown and straight, and that she was taller than he was and had freckles. Their personalities were different too.

"We don't look alike because we're not *identical* twins," she explained. "We're fraternal—brother and sister, born at the same time."

"How old are you?" asked Jack.

"Almost ten," said the twins.

"Do you have any allergies?"

"No."

"Chronic illnesses?"

"No."

"Criminal records?"

"What?" yelped Tessa. "Of course not. Why are you asking us all these questions? All we want to do is rent some pans!"

"I . . . have to be very careful with my merchandise," said Jack hastily. "But it's all right—you can take the pans. Just return them by seven tomorrow. We close at seven."

"Doesn't the mall stay open until nine?" asked Tod. He looked around, hoping to see some other interesting gadgets. Maybe Gemini Jack had something he could use for the science fair.

"I close early because . . . I'm taking a class," said Jack.

Beep beep.

"What's that?" asked Tessa, still a little rattled by Jack's questions. The beep reminded her of her Chinese watch, a gift from her mother that beeped every hour on the hour. Tessa liked the sound—it made her feel efficient—but Lou and Lulu didn't, so she'd stopped wearing it.

Jack reached under the counter and pulled out a

little pink electronic pet. There was a smiling face on its tiny LCD screen, with round eyes that seemed to look right at Tessa.

"Oh! She's adorable!" exclaimed Tessa, who had always wanted an electronic pet. This one was especially pretty. Its radiant face looked almost alive. "Does she have a name?"

"How do you know it's a she?" asked Tod. He hated electronic pets. He hadn't liked Tessa's beeping watch much either.

"I can tell," said Tessa. "Look at her eyelashes!" The pet's eyelashes were long and curly.

Tod groaned.

"Her name is FM," said Jack, dropping the little device into Tessa's hand.

"FM?" Tessa could hardly take her eyes off the little e-pet. There was something irresistible about it. The last time Tod had seen that expression on his sister's face was when she got her plush pony, which she still kept on her bed. This was definitely love at first sight.

"Short for Fib Muncher," said Jack. "She eats lies. They are like . . . candy to her."

"Don't rent her, Tessa," said Tod. "Those things are a major pain—you have to feed them and change them and take care of them all day. Besides, Mr. Harken banned them, remember?"

Tod's reminder about the principal's ban had no effect on Tessa, who was staring lovingly at FM's face.

"You don't have to rent her," said Jack. "You can take her for a day. She likes to get out and around. Just keep her fed."

"On fibs?" said Tod. For the first time he smiled. "That shouldn't be a problem."

"Thanks! Thanks so much!" cried Tessa. She felt a little strange about taking the e-pet from Jack and not paying for it. On the other hand, she'd be back the next day to return the pans, so she guessed it was okay. Tod grabbed the shopping bag and followed her out of the store.

"That place is *weird*," he said. "And the guy, Gemini Jack? Am I wrong, or did he have too many fingers?"

"You're not wrong," said Tessa. "And did you notice his mouth? Bizarre!" she exclaimed, using one of their father's favorite expressions.

Tod shook his head, then nodded, looking just slightly dazed. "Mmm-hmm," he said, "I did. I still can't really believe that it appears when he talks and disappears when—"

"Hold it. Don't move!" said a gruff voice. A pair of heavy hands came down on the twins' shoulders. "You're under arrest!"

chapter 4

Startled, Tessa swung around.

"Gotcha!" said a ponytailed young man in a blue uniform, looking pleased with himself.

"Watson! That is so not funny!" she said.

The man stood there with an exaggerated look of innocence on his face. "Just kidding! Just kidding," he said, raising his hands. "But you have to admit the line's a great attention-getter."

Watson was the security guard at Middle Valley Middle School. He had gone to Middle Valley himself, years ago, and he was known at the school for two things—telling dumb jokes and hiding in the utility closet during school hours. The rumor was that he was writing a comedy routine in there. Watson's ambition was to be a stand-up comedian.

"What are you doing here?" asked Tod.

"Moonlighting," said Watson. "Mall security, hall security. Can *you* tell the difference? I can't. By the way, where's your bathroom pass?"

"Watson!" exclaimed Tessa. "This is the mall, not the school. We don't need passes here."

He cackled. "Gotcha again!"

Tessa rolled her eyes. She could tell Watson was just warming up.

"Did you hear the one about the duck who was so funny he quacked himself up?" asked the guard. Tod snorted. He actually thought Watson was funny.

Tessa pulled at her brother's sleeve. "Come on," she said. "We've got to go."

"Bye, Watson," said Tod. "See you in school."

"Hey!" called Watson as they jumped on the escalator. "How do crazy people get through the forest? They take the psycho . . ." His voice faded away as they glided down.

"He is *such* a cornball," said Tessa when they were safely out of his range. "I feel like I should wear joke repellent around him."

Tod snapped his fingers. "Psychopath," he murmured. "Not bad."

As they stepped off the escalator, Tessa hesitated for a moment. "Speaking of bad," she said, indicating the front entrance, "there it is in dupli-cate."

Ned and Nancy Gneiss, the only other twins at Middle Valley Middle School, were standing at the doors with a shopping bag between them. Their name was pronounced "nice," but they were any-thing but. Tessa thought of them as Notso and Never.

"Oh. Very bad," said Tod. He disliked them too. They were neat, clean, scheming, and creepy, though most adults didn't seem to notice the schem-ing, creepy parts. Right now, unfortunately, the Gneiss twins couldn't be avoided.

"Hi," muttered Tod and Tessa.

"Hi," said Nancy and Ned. Ned was playing with a toothpick, impaling jelly beans on it and then popping them into his mouth.

"Got your science project finished?" he asked Tod, chewing. They both had Mr. Brock, the sci-ence teacher who was in charge of the fair.

"Uh—" began Tod.

"Sure!" said Tessa.

Beep beep.

"What's that stupid noise?" asked Nancy. She glared at Tessa.

"Egg timer," said Tod.

"Alarm clock," said Tessa at the same moment. Neither of them wanted to tell the Gneiss twins about Gemini Jack's.

Beep beep, said FM. *Beep beep.*

Tod and Tessa looked at each other quickly. FM was beeping because they were lying! For a moment even Tessa was speechless. The pet really was a Fib Muncher! Amazing!

At the same time, she realized that she and Tod would have to be very careful about what they said to the Gneiss twins. Ned and Nancy were creepy, but they weren't stupid.

"What'd you buy?" Tessa asked quickly, indicating their shopping bag.

"Plant food," said Nancy.

"Bungee cords," said Ned.

Beep beep, said FM. *Beep beep!*

"Hey! What's that—?" Nancy began, but at that moment a station wagon pulled up at the curb, and the thin, dark-haired woman at the wheel honked the horn and waved.

"There's Mom," said Ned, flicking his toothpick away.

"Gotta run," said Nancy. Ned picked up the shopping bag and hurried to the car.

"Did you see that bag?" Tod said to Tessa. "It was from Techno Toys."

"So?"

"Bet Ned was *buying* his science fair project," said Tod.

"That's not allowed, is it?"

"Like he cares," said Tod. "Brock turned down his first idea, which was really gross—a display of live butterflies, pinned to a board."

"Ugh," said Tessa.

"Ugh is right. Ned wanted to time how long it would take them to die. Brock told him he had to do a cruelty-free project. Turns out Ned already had the board and the butterfly net and everything. He was steamed."

"One thing's for sure," said Tessa. "Both of them were lying like rugs. Look."

FM's little eyes were closed in a smile of pure bliss.

"We lied too," said Tod.

"Mmm. Look how sweet she is," said Tessa, sighing fondly.

Tod shot his sister a look. "Let's go," he said, unlocking his bike. "Lulu's waiting for these pans."

chapter 5

"**T**hanks!" said Lulu, looking into the shopping bag. "This is great, you guys." But when she tried to pull out the pans, they slipped through her fingers, clattered to the floor, bounced back up, and whizzed halfway across the kitchen, hitting the rocking chair and setting it in violent motion. Ronette, the big Persian cat dozing on the cushion, found herself launched into space. She yowled in shock.

It all happened so quickly that the twins' "You're welcome" was followed by a loud "Yikes!" as the pans, now giant berserk hockey pucks, whipped across the floor at Mach 2. Meanwhile Ronette landed hard. She hissed furiously at everyone before running out of the kitchen, moving very fast for such a hefty animal.

"Holy moly!" exclaimed Lulu, laughing in amazement.

Tessa looked at Tod. "Remember what he called them?" she asked.

"Guaranteed one hundred percent friction free," said Tod. "Uh-oh."

Lulu bent down and tried to grab a pan. It slithered away as soon as she touched it. "Kids!" she exclaimed. "Tell me I'm not hallucinating! Where did you *get* these things?"

Tod mumbled "Rental store" and Tessa said "The mall," hoping Lulu wouldn't press them. Then they got down on the floor for a quick parley about strategy.

"What if we try to grab it really fast?"

"How about really slowly?" said Tod.

"Let's see if we can slip our hands under it," said Tessa, thinking of how she'd once held a newborn goat.

"Okay." They inched their hands along the pine floor and under the pan. It slipped and slid a little but allowed itself to be picked up—very, very slowly. The twins set the pan on the counter. It stayed there, and everybody sighed with relief.

"I guess they're touchy," said Lulu. "I had a temperamental frying pan once. Hated onions. Always burned them. Cooked everything else perfectly." She knelt and picked up the other pans the way the twins had. "I'll just handle them extra-carefully," she said when they were lined up in a row.

Then she lit the oven. Tod, satisfied that things were under control, mumbled something about his science project and disappeared. Tessa sat down in the rocker with a glass of lemonade and watched Lulu's transformation.

It was a rapid change, from slow, mellow, friendly grandmother to zippy, efficient, no-nonsense food professional, and it took place whenever Lulu had a cooking job. The rule was that Tessa could stick around and watch—if she kept quiet. "Idle chatter angers the kitchen gods," Lulu liked to say.

Tessa wasn't sure if she was serious, but she kept quiet, because she loved to watch her grandmother cook. As she began working Lulu would fall silent, tie her long hair back in a knot, and wash her hands. Then she would turn to her ingredients, handling them with the speed and precision of a surgeon performing a complex procedure.

This afternoon, thought Tessa, it was Operation Oh Wow.

All the ingredients for the bread pudding were

arranged neatly on the counter. There were three stacks of freshly baked, buttered bread slices, a bowl full of milky stuff that smelled of vanilla, a shaker of chocolate sprinkles, and a dish of candied orange peel.

Humming tunelessly, Lulu lined each pan with bread. She peered inside the oven and checked the temperature, using an ancient flashlight, then poured the milky stuff into the pans until each pan held exactly the same amount. She decorated the puddings with big, scrawly zigzags of chocolate sprinkles, then dotted them with little clumps of orange peel.

The pans were ready to go into the oven.

Tessa jumped up to help. Together she and Lulu picked up the pans from underneath. Moving in slow motion, they placed them in the oven side by side.

After Lulu set the timer she said "There!" and smiled at Tessa. Suddenly she was the other, relaxed Lulu again. "So," she said, licking her fingers, "have fun at the mall?"

"Sure," said Tessa. "All we did was get the pans, though."

"Those pans are really something," said Lulu, shaking her head. "I don't mean to criticize, sweetie, but they could be a little easier to use. Where'd you get them?"

"Some store called Gemini Jack's," said Tessa. She wasn't sure why, but she didn't want to say too much about Jack or his store. "Just a regular old store," she added.

Beep beep, FM piped up from Tessa's backpack.

"What's that?" asked Lulu, frowning at the electronic sound. "Are you wearing that watch again? I thought you felt relaxed enough to put it away. You don't have to worry about timetables and schedules around here, you know that, don't you?"

"It was nothing," said Tessa.

Beep beep!

"I mean it wasn't my watch." Tessa grabbed her pack and was out the door before Lulu had a chance to ask any more questions.

At exactly 7:01 a low electronic hum sounded behind the locked doors of Gemini Jack's U Rent All. Jack, sitting alone in the dark of the store, responded to the signal by pressing three buttons on the counter, touching a tiny indentation above his right ear, and clearing his throat.

A square of iridescent light appeared on the wall

behind the counter, followed by his twin's holographic image. As usual, she looked serious.

"Great news!" he told her. "A unit came in today—on my first day!"

Jill's expression did not change. "Are they suitable?" she asked.

"I'm not one hundred percent sure," said Jack. "But they're coming back tomorrow. I'll find out."

"May I remind you that we are in a hurry?" said Jill. She was not the most patient being on their double planet. "And we don't just need just *any* unit. We need a unit that is young, ruthless, cold-blooded, aggressive, dishonest, and wily. These are characteristics that abound on Earth."

"Yes, I know," said Jack, thinking that Tessa and Tod didn't quite fit Jill's description. He tended to be more optimistic than his twin, so he wasn't ready to dismiss them yet.

"I'm testing them," he told her. "I loaned them an FM. I'll know a lot more tomorrow when I see the condition she's in. Or if she's alive at all."

"Tomorrow, then," said Jill. "Remember, everyone is counting on us. On you." Her unsmiling image disappeared.

chapter 6

"What'd you do with FM?" Tod asked Tessa on their way to school the next morning.

"You mean Effie?" That was Tessa's name for the little electronic pet. "I, uh, left her back in my room."

Beep beep. The sound came from Tessa's pack.

"Sure you did," said Tod.

"Okay, okay," said Tessa. "I just couldn't stand to leave her behind." The night before, while she played with Effie, Tessa had learned that the little e-pet responded to more than just lies. She would blink and smile when Tessa said hello. She would bat her eyelashes when Tessa said "Girls rule." And when Tessa told a really outrageous lie ("I think I have a crush on Ned Gneiss"), Effie practically squawked, almost as if she were laughing.

One of Tod's eyebrows went up. Had Tessa been this goofy about the plush pony? He didn't think so. "You know Harken's rule," he said. "He's gonna confiscate her."

Tessa knew very well that the principal didn't allow pets—live or electronic. She was nervous about breaking the rule too. But she had Effie for only a few more hours! It would be hard enough later, when she had to return the pet to Jack. "I'll keep her in my pack," she told her brother. "All I have to do is feed her."

"How?"

Tessa smiled mischievously. "I hate Effie," she said loudly. "So I won't feed her anything but slimy dead bugs."

A bouncy little *Beep beep!* came from Tessa's pack. Tessa sighed with pleasure. "See how smart she is?" she said. "She knows I love her!"

Tod shook his head. They were a block from the schoolyard, at the big oak tree on the corner, so they said goodbye and Tessa ran ahead to join her friends Lisa and Lissa.

Tod stood under the tree for a moment, wishing he could go back to the ranch and work on his science project. Now that he'd fixed the propeller and attached it to the toy car axle, it was time to work on the motor—the best part. A squirrel chittered at him from a branch, as if reminding him of the time.

"Okay, okay," said Tod. A few minutes later he was in his first-period class, English. He never found it too interesting, but today it was especially boring and slow because it was spelling and grammar. The Gneiss twins kept holding everything up because they couldn't spell.

Second period was math. For Tod that was a big improvement over English. Not that it was easy—fractions were hard. But Tod liked doing them.

Third period was science, Tod's favorite. He liked the subject, and he liked the teacher. Mr. Brock used to be a drama teacher, but after drama was cut from the curriculum because of something to do with taxes, he'd been assigned to science. Some parents complained because he didn't know science too well anymore—he hadn't taught it in all the years he'd been teaching drama—but the kids liked him. If he got something wrong, Tod or one of the other science brains would correct him. No matter how politely they did it, Brock would groan, slam himself on the forehead, and pretend to fall backward. Sometimes he would shout " 'O, I die, Horatio!' " in a really tragic voice, which always made them laugh.

Plus, Brock wore an earring, which Tod thought was cool.

"A week until the science fair," Mr. Brock said as the class began.

"Two!" shouted the class.

" 'O, what a noble mind is here o'erthrown!' " declaimed Mr. Brock. Then he added in a normal voice, "I hope all of you will have your projects ready."

Tod noticed that everybody was nodding except Ned.

"And remember," said Mr. Brock. "We want to be able to certify that no living beings were harmed in the making of our science fair."

"Why's that such a big deal? What's the point?" said Ned.

"I'll ignore that, Ned," said Mr. Brock. "Now, where were we?" he asked.

"Surface tension, Mr. Brock," came a chorus of voices.

Tessa was not in Tod's science class; she was in her third-period civics class with Ms. Blitz. Ms. Blitz did not clown around and shout lines from Shakespeare. She was much too serious for that. She talked a lot about the importance of being a good citizen, and having an interest in public affairs, and because her voice sounded like a mower cutting grass on some far-off lawn, Tessa found it hard to pay attention to her.

Today, however, Ms. Blitz was pretty keyed up. She had invited an important guest to speak—Mayor Bryce Palmetto—and he had accepted. Now here he was in her classroom. Ms. Blitz's expression made it clear that she wanted everybody to pay very close attention to the mayor.

Mayor Palmetto was tall and reed-thin. He had a habit of smiling quickly when he finished a sentence, as if the smile were punctuation. He had done this when he was introduced, and he was doing it now, as he talked about tax reform.

"With this new program in place," he said, "we will not only lower taxes, but also improve the schools."

Beep beep. The noise came from the floor, where Tessa had set her pack. Oh, no! thought Tessa. "Shut up, Effie!" she whispered.

"Due to the higher number of students in each class," continued the mayor, "social interaction will increase and intensify. This virtually guarantees an enriched educational experience for all."

Beep beep!

Ms. Blitz scowled at the class. "What was that noise?" she demanded, looking in Tessa's direction.

"Nothing," said Tessa. She shrugged.

Beep BEEP! Suddenly Effie sounded very loud. The classroom fell silent, and even Mr. Palmetto stopped talking.

Tessa swallowed, feeling dread.

"Tessa Gibson!" snapped Ms. Blitz. "Come up here at once! And bring your backpack with you!"

chapter 7

*T*essa was never late. So where was she? Tod stood at the tree on the corner and peered down the street. No Tessa. Five minutes went by, then another five. He kept expecting her to come racing up to him, red hair flying, but she didn't.

Tod wondered if she was in detention. Strangely enough, it was a possibility. Not for cheating or smoking or chewing gum, of course—she would never do any of that. But she did expect people to be honest and fair, and when they weren't, she had a bad habit of calling them on it. This had gotten her detention more than once.

Tod knew when to be quiet. That was another way the twins were different.

After waiting another five minutes, he walked back to school and peeked into the library, which served as detention hall. Sure enough, there was Tessa. She was leafing through one of her beloved horse books. Even so, she looked unhappy. Tod decided to wait for her. He settled against the wall outside the library and started to do his math homework. Detention would be over soon.

But when it was, Tessa was out of the library so fast that he had to scramble to his feet and run after her.

"Hey!" he called, catching up with her at the other end of the hall. "Slow down. Where are you going?"

"Mr. Harken's office," she told him, her normally cheerful mouth twisting into a worried line. "They took Effie. And don't you dare say 'I told you so.'"

"I told you so," Tod whispered. To himself.

He followed Tessa into the principal's office. The outer office, a large, sunny reception area, was full of kids—fifth-graders, sixth-graders, even a few seventh-graders. They were all girls, and they were all sniffling, sobbing, or wailing.

Tod had never heard anything like it. Mr. Harken, looking grim, stood behind the big desk in his office. His assistant, Ms. Herman, was trying to help Watson untangle himself from a big ball of yellow CRIME SCENE tape. Watson's security guard cap was on crooked, and his wispy blond ponytail had come undone.

"What's going on?" Tessa asked one of the snifflers.

"My pet—" began the girl, and then broke down, becoming a sobber.

"Her e-pet," said another girl, tears spilling out of her round brown eyes. "It's gone!"

"Gone?" Tessa blinked rapidly and turned pale. "I thought we were supposed to get them back at the end of the day!"

"Gone!" sobbed a seventh-grader, wiping smeared mascara from under her eyes. "You know how Mr. Harken keeps all the confiscated pets in a drawer?"

Tessa nodded.

"Somebody stole them!"

"Stole the whole drawerful!" exclaimed the girl with brown eyes as tears streamed down her cheeks. "They're all gone. They'll starve! They'll die!"

That explained Watson's presence, thought Tod. He was probably looking for clues.

"Oh, no!" moaned Tessa. "Effie!"

Ms. Herman came out of Mr. Harken's office. She was a roundish woman with a singsong voice who had once taught kindergarten, and she still talked to people as if they were five years old—even Mr. Harken.

"Boys and gir-ruls," she called. "The principal would like you to leave now. Our security officer can't do his work with all this commotion."

"But—but what about my pet?" wailed the seventh-grader. "I feel like I've lost a dog or a cat!"

"Only worse!" sobbed the girl with brown eyes.

"We'll let you know as soon as we have any news," said Ms. Herman soothingly. "Now go on home. School is over for today."

The group filed out. Tod turned to Tessa. "You know, we have to return the pans to Gemini Jack."

"We'll have to tell him Effie's gone," Tessa said gloomily. She wasn't sniffling or crying. It wasn't her style. But Tod knew she was really upset. Even her freckles looked pale.

As they left the office he noticed a folded note taped to the back of the door. There was a message on it:

E-limenate E-pets E-meddiately!

"Hey, look at this," said Tod. "Maybe it's a ransom note." He pulled it down and started to unfold it.

"Now, Tod, that's evidence," scolded Ms. Herman. She took the note from Tod before he could read much more than the name William Shakespeare on it. A Shakespeare quote? thought Tod. That's strange.

"It has to go to the authorities." Ms. Herman handed it to Watson, who wiggled his eyebrows teasingly at the twins.

"But—" Tod really wanted to read the note.

"But—" So did Tessa.

"Skedaddle, you two," said Ms. Herman, showing them the door. They had no choice but to leave.

"Did you read it?" Tessa asked Tod when they were in the hallway.

"I couldn't," he said. "But I did see something strange before Herman grabbed it. I think there's a quote from Shakespeare in the note."

"Huh," said Tessa. "That *is* strange."

"And something else," said Tod.

"What?"

"I can't remember."

"So, how was school today, kids?" asked Mrs. Gneiss through her tears. She was cutting onions into chunks at the kitchen counter.

"Fine." The twins usually stayed out of the

kitchen, but tonight Mrs. Gneiss was making kebabs, so they were helping.

"Some stuff got stolen," said Ned, sticking a skewer through half a dozen cubes of lamb. "Looks like a teacher did it."

"Oh? What was stolen?"

"Only a bunch of stupid e-pets," said Ned.

"What are they?" asked Mrs. Gneiss.

"Stupid whiny little things," said Nancy, skewering some meat energetically. "Some girls like them."

Mrs. Gneiss frowned. "Put vegetables on the kebab, too," she said. "Not just meat."

"Vegetables are no fun," said Ned. "They don't bleed." When he saw her worried expression he added, "Just kidding, Mom. Joke."

Nancy snickered.

Mrs. Gneiss's eyes filled with tears. She blew her nose. "Onions," she said by way of explanation to the twins.

There were times when her children almost frightened her.

chapter 8

As he fed the goats and watered the baby vegetables, Tod thought about the folded note he'd noticed in Mr. Harken's office. In the kitchen, as he got ready to feed Ronette and Shirelle, he thought about it some more.

The two cats, who were as round and heavy as bowling balls, came at him as he opened their cans of organic cat food, hitting his legs so hard that they nearly knocked him over. Their urgent meowing sounded just like the girls crying in Mr. Harken's office.

As Tod set the cats' dishes on the floor, he finally realized what had struck him about the note.

That's it! he thought. At that very moment, Tessa charged into the kitchen calling his name, and the connecting thought, the one that linked the e-pets and the Shakespeare quote to another, more important clue, flew away like a startled bird.

"Help me collect some watercress!" Tessa came to a screeching halt when she saw the frown on her brother's face. "What?" she asked.

"I had it and I lost it," he said. "The thing about the note."

"You'll remember," said Tessa, heading for the stream.

"Mmmph," mumbled Tod, following. Not being able to remember was annoying, like losing a nut or a bolt or some small, important part of a machine he was fixing.

By the time they got back to the kitchen with the watercress, the table was set. Lou, wearing his wire-rimmed spectacles on his broad forehead, was dicing cheese for the pizza. His big hands moved deftly.

"All the baby goats are in great shape. And so is Yoko," he said, referring to their mother. "She sang harmony on 'Good Vibrations' tonight."

"That's a groove," said Lulu. Lou claimed that the goats sang along with the jukebox when he milked them, and Lulu humored him.

Half an hour later they were at the table, their faces golden in the early-evening light. "Whose turn is it?" asked Lou.

"Mine," said Lulu. They took turns saying grace, which they were allowed to make up. "As long as it's a good, positive thought," Lulu liked to say, "we can use it."

At first Tod had been embarrassed by Lou and Lulu's dinnertime ritual. His parents never said grace. Their dinners were brisk and lively—with nonstop talk about news, business, and school.

But over the years Tod had come to like the slow, quiet dinners at the ranch, and now he didn't mind saying grace, especially since the food at Lou and Lulu's was so good.

Today, however, he was glad it wasn't his turn. He'd have a hard time calling up a positive thought, because he was worried about what he and Tessa would tell Jack about FM, and he was worried about being late. Jack had told them to be there by seven, and it was six already.

They bowed their heads. Lulu said, "Thank you for the babies in the barn, the seedlings in the garden, and the energy to nurture them all."

"Amen, and let's eat!" said Lou.

And then nobody said anything for a few minutes—Lou because he was hungry, and Lulu because she was concentrating on the pizza. It was a new recipe, and she ate it as if she were reading a mystery for clues.

Tod and Tessa had their own reasons for being quiet. They were going to be late getting to Jack's; the clock over the stove said 6:30.

"Can we be excused?" asked Tessa.

"Only one piece of pizza?" said Lulu. "Aren't you hungry?"

"Sure," said Tod.

"No," said Tessa at exactly the same time.

One of Lou's eyebrows went up. "Anything wrong?" he asked.

"Not a thing," said Tod.

"Right. No," said Tessa, who hated to lie. She almost wished Effie were there to beep at her, and this was such an upsetting thought that she choked on her iced tea.

A few more questions, thought Tod as Lulu clapped Tessa on the back, and Lou and Lulu would be treated to a full description of the Gemini Jack/Effie/e-pet crisis. As much as he loved his grandparents, he didn't think they were ready for that.

He stood. "We have to return the pans by seven," he said to Tessa. "We only rented them for a day, remember?"

"Right!" said Tessa, leaping up. "We'd better get

there before the store closes." The pans were in the Gemini Jack's shopping bag next to the counter. Tessa grabbed the bag and headed for the door.

"Isn't the mall closed already?" asked Lulu. "It's six-thirty-five."

"Malls stay open late," Tod told her. The things his grandmother didn't know amazed him.

"Weird," she commented, which was her way of expressing disapproval.

"Be back by eight," said Lou as the screen door slammed behind the twins. "It's a school night."

"Okay!" They hurried away.

chapter 9

The music in the mall that evening was soft and quiet, not bouncy and cheerful the way it had been during their first visit. There weren't many shoppers around. And the stars in the ceiling were twinkling slowly, as if they were running out of energy. The hushed feeling made Tod just a little nervous.

"Hold it right there!" ordered a gruff voice. Tod spun around. But it was only Watson. "Question for you," said the guard, following the twins onto the escalator. "What do prisoners use to call each other?"

Sometimes Tessa pretended not to know Watson's jokes, but tonight she wasn't in the mood. "Cell phones," she snapped.

Watson's face fell. "How'd you know?" he asked.

"Everybody knows that one, Watson," said Tod.

"Well, how about this," said Watson. "Why did the hubcap take a nap?"

"I'm stumped," said Tod politely.

"Because he was tired!" crowed Watson. The twins smiled. They'd heard that joke in second grade.

"You're a tough crowd, you know that?" said the guard. "Even Mr. Harken laughed at that one."

Hearing the principal's name reminded Tod of the ransom note. "Here's a question for you, Watson," he said.

"Hit me!"

"What happened to the note I found this afternoon? The one in Mr. Harken's office?"

Clever Tod, thought Tessa.

The guard looked puzzled. "Is that a joke?" he asked. "That's not a joke."

"No," admitted Tod. "I just wondered."

"Ah, I think Ms. Herman has it," said Watson. "Not sure. Anyway, I probably shouldn't talk about the case. It's kind of sensitive, because of the Shakespeare quote and Mr. Brock and everything. . . ."

"Mr. Brock?" said Tod.

"Never mind," said Watson. "Top secret. Now, here's a question for you. How do you get a hanky to dance?"

"Easy," said the twins. "You put a little boogie in it." They raced up the escalator to Level 3.

"We shouldn't have spent so much time with Watson," said Tessa as they reached Level 3. "But maybe we're not late. The stores up here are still open." She looked around for Gemini Jack's. "Was it at this end? Or the other?"

"I can't remember," said Tod.

Tessa saw that the clock in the Home Office Depot window said 7:03. They were late. "Maybe we should walk backwards again," she said, doing just that. She took one step, then another.

Nothing happened.

"I think we have to hold hands," she said.

"Oh, all right." Tod took her hand.

"There!" she cried, pointing.

Tod turned. There were the bright letters, reflected in the Home Office Depot window:

GEMINI JACK'S U RENT ALL
Be First in the Universe!

The sign blinked on, then off.

Bong! went the door when they opened it.

Jack was taking down the ONE FREE FOR TWO SALE

sign. "Sorry," he told them, shaking his head. "We're closed."

"Closed?" said Tessa. "But we're returning the pans."

"It's after seven," said Jack. "I told you to be here by seven. I have to close. I have reports to—I mean, things to do."

"Sorry," said Tod. "We kind of got held up."

"We really hurried so we wouldn't be late," said Tessa. "But the guard stopped us." She looked pleadingly at Jack, who was watching her closely.

"I see you are genuinely sorry," he said, sounding oddly disappointed.

Tessa nodded. "Oh, all right. Just this once," said Jack, pressing a square indentation set into the counter. "I'll hit Back."

"Hit back?" The twins looked at Jack, alarmed. Was he going to strike them? Then suddenly they were back in the corridor outside Jack's door.

The clock in the Home Office Depot window said 6:51. They opened Jack's door. It bonged.

"That's better," said Jack as they walked in. "You just made it."

"What happened?" asked the twins.

"I hit Back," said Jack, indicating the indentation in the counter. "It's a one-event Back, but that's usually enough."

"Wow," said Tod. "Can we rent that?"

Jack shook his head. "Employees only. Ah!" he said. "I see you have the pans."

"Oh, right. Here," said Tod, handing over the shopping bag.

"Very good. And FM? Fib Muncher? Did she enjoy her visit to your world, I mean the world?"

There was a short silence. "Well . . ." Tessa looked at the floor.

"We don't know yet," said Tod.

"Why not?" asked Jack.

"There's . . . a problem," said Tessa.

"There's . . . a mix-up," said Tod at the same moment.

"Wait. Stop. One at a time, please," said Jack. "What's the problem?"

Tessa swallowed. Then she told him about the e-pet abduction.

"I see you feel very bad about this, also," said Jack as the twins nodded. "That's unfortunate—I mean, the situation is unfortunate."

"I'm sorry," said Tessa. "I'll bring her back as soon

as we get her, I promise. The guard or the police will find her and—"

"Guard? Police? Didn't you tell me *you* found the ransom note?"

"Actually, it was Tod," said Tessa.

"Do you have any confidence in these . . . officials?" asked Jack.

"Not a lot."

"Not a whole lot."

"Hardly any."

"None at all."

"Then I hope you will recover Fib Muncher yourselves," said Jack.

"We want to," said Tessa, "but how?"

"Use clues," said Jack. "There are always clues when there's a crime. It's a law of the universe."

"There was a clue," said Tod. "The note. But we weren't allowed to see it."

"Hmmm," said Jack. His eyes closed and a low thrum, like the sound of an engine turning over, came out of his mouth.

"What?" asked the twins.

"Nothing," said Jack. "Just thinking out loud." He reached under the counter and brought up a little black plastic device. It was rectangular and flat and could have passed for a candy bar or a small remote control.

"I'll rent you this for a day or so," he said. "It will help you get FM back. But you have to promise to be very careful with it."

"I promise," said Tod.

"Me too," said Tessa. "What is it?"

"It's a Do Right," said Jack. "First you point it at someone. Then you let them know what you want them to do."

"And then what?" asked Tessa.

"Then they do it," said Jack.

"Really?" asked the twins together.

"Really. But it has to be a suggestion, not a command. And it only works on half a unit—I mean one person—at a time."

"Yowza," said Tod. "Where do you *get* all this cool stuff?" A gadget like the Do Right would be awesome for the science fair, he thought.

Jack stiffened slightly. "I'm afraid we can't tell you that," he said.

We? wondered Tessa.

"Make sure this doesn't fall into the wrong hands," said Jack, handing the Do Right to Tod. "It cannot be lost and must be returned."

"O-*kay*," said Tod. "Will do."

"What's the rental fee?" asked Tessa as the twins reached the door. "For the Do Right, I mean."

"You're in luck," said Jack. "It was part of the one-free-for-two sale. The Do Right comes with the pans. There's absolutely no charge for it."

chapter 10

*J*ack closed up shop the instant the twins were gone. When the signal came at 7:01, he was ready.

His twin's image appeared. As usual, her expression was grave. "Any luck?" she asked.

"Afraid not," said Jack.

"That's too bad," she said. "Remember the rumor that the Vorons were massing? It's true."

Jack flinched, though he wasn't really surprised. The Vorons, always intent on suppression and domination, were usually on the attack somewhere. They were bound to target Gemini sooner or later.

In the past Jack's planet could have defended itself. But the last few centuries had seen a strange change on Gemini, a loss of vitality that had left Jack's species weak, passive, and unable to fight. It was the kind of change that brought disaster, once the rest of the galaxy found out.

And that was beginning to happen. The Vorons would be the first to challenge Gemini. If they didn't succeed, some other, even stronger enemy would.

Earth was the only planet other than Jack's own that boasted twin life-forms. They were in the minority here, but that didn't matter—they made up for it with their aggression. Human aggression was famed throughout the universe. All Jack needed was a DNA sample from one young, strong, ruthless human unit. The sample had to be the old-fashioned nasty stuff—without a trace of compassion, honesty, or niceness. Once introduced on Gemini, the sample would work like a supersteroid—pumping up his species and giving it the defensive energy it lacked.

"What about the unit you found?" asked Jill. "Did they return the FM?"

"No."

"Good! Perhaps they are the ones we want." For an instant her morose face looked hopeful.

"No," Jack said again. "It was stolen from them. They didn't torture or destroy it." He sighed. "At least the Vorons are slow," he said. "They'll take Earth-weeks to reach us."

"But they will reach us," Jill insisted darkly.

There was a painful silence as Jack and his twin thought about the imminent doom of their planet.

"Keep trying. Please," Jill said then. "There must be a nasty unit somewhere that will serve our purposes."

Jack nodded as Jill broke contact and disappeared.

"Gemini Jack is really, really weird," said Tod late that night.

"Mmm. He is," Tessa agreed drowsily.

"He's so weird," Tod continued, "that . . . I think he might be from another planet." They were in their adjoining rooms in the attic. There was no door between them, just a beaded curtain, so they had privacy when they needed it but could talk when they wanted to.

Tessa's eyes flew open. "Really? Why do you think so?"

"Remember when I asked him where he got all the cool stuff and he wouldn't tell? Aliens are always trying to hide the fact that they're aliens. Besides, he looks like an alien," said Tod. "He has way too many fingers."

Tessa hadn't counted Jack's fingers, but his skin—so smooth it reminded her of pearly nail polish—

had definitely made an impression on her. "What if he's from another time, like the future?"

"Nope."

"How do you know?" she asked, wondering how Tod could be so sure.

"From science fiction movies," said Tod, wondering how Tessa could be so clueless. "Whenever anybody's from the future, they always say so right away. They can't keep it to themselves—it's like, 'Look at me, I'm ahead of you.' But aliens are the opposite. They're always secretive and pretending to be human."

"Well, if he is an alien, and not from the future, what's he up to? Is he part of some evil plot to take over the earth?" she asked jokingly. Tessa didn't believe Jack was evil. After all, he'd loaned her Effie.

"Could be," said Tod.

"*Really?*"

"It's possible," said Tod. "He seems nice, and he's acting like he wants to help us. But there could be a reason for that—something we don't know about."

"Like a hidden agenda?" said Tessa, using a phrase of their mother's.

"Right," said Tod, yawning. "But he could be harmless, too. Maybe his mission is peaceful." Actually, Jack made Tod nervous, though he'd never

admit that to Tessa. He had to draw the line somewhere.

They talked about Jack for a while, and then they
talked about what they were going to do the next
day. There was only one clue, and only one way to
get it, so the plan was simple.

When they met at the principal's office at three-
thirty the following afternoon, they were both nervous. And quiet.

The school was quiet too. The resounding boom
of hundreds of kids hurtling out of the building had
faded away, and now the twins heard only the dis-
tant whine of the janitor's vacuum and the ticking
of the old windup clock on Ms. Herman's desk.

"My goodness, children!" she exclaimed when
she noticed them. "You startled me, coming in here
so quietly. What is it?"

"Is Mr. Harken in?" asked Tod.

"I'm afraid he's busy right now," said Ms. Herman. A loud snort, and then another, came from
behind the principal's glass-paneled door. Tessa recognized the sound. Some grown-ups made it when
they fell asleep sitting in a chair.

"About the note," said Tod. "Do you still have
it?"

"That's an official matter," said Ms. Herman with a quick glance down at her desk drawer. Aha! thought Tessa. She pointed the Do Right at Ms. Herman and pressed the button.

"Give us the note!" she said, feeling a little silly.

Ms. Herman looked at her blankly without moving.

"It has to be a suggestion," Tod reminded Tessa.

She gasped. She'd forgotten. "Um, why not give us the note, Ms. Herman?" she asked softly.

"Good idea," said Ms. Herman, opening her drawer. She pulled out a piece of paper and handed it to Tessa, who was just about to thank her when Tod grabbed the Do Right.

"Why don't you make a copy of the note?" he said to Ms. Herman. "That way you can keep the original. And we won't get in trouble over a missing note," he added for his sister's benefit.

"Great idea!" Tessa gave him a thumbs-up.

"Great idea," echoed Ms. Herman, getting up to run the note through the copier. She handed the copy to Tod, then settled back into her chair looking slightly dazed.

"And how about forgetting about our conversation this afternoon?" suggested Tod, using the Do Right again.

"*Good* idea," said Ms. Herman as they backed out of the office. Tessa closed the door.

"Hold it right there!"

"Oh, no," groaned Tessa. It was Watson.

"Hey, kids," said the guard. "Did you hear the one about the mushroom who got invited to all the parties, because he was such a—"

Tessa pointed the Do Right at Watson. "Excuse me," she said softly, "but weren't you on your way to the utility closet? To work on your comedy routine?"

Watson stopped in his tracks. "Good idea," he said.

"And today, why not write a funny joke?" suggested Tessa. "One that actually makes people laugh."

Watson nodded. "Yeah!" he said. "*Good* idea." Wheeling, he headed toward the utility closet at the end of the hall.

"If the Do Right can't make him do it, nothing can," said Tessa.

chapter 11

They jumped onto their bikes and raced away. When they were half a mile from school they high-fived each other and Tessa pulled the ransom note out of her pack.

They read it together.

E-limenate E-pets E-meddiately!
E-pet Owners Be-Ware!
"HERE IS MY JURNEY'S END, HERE IS MY BUTT."
—W. Shakespeer

WE WILL STARVE YOUR E-PETS
AND LET THEM DIE!
THEN STICK THEM WITH SHARP INSTERMENTS!

Tessa's face turned white. "Starve them? Stick them?" she moaned. "Oh, no! This is worse than I thought! It's terrible! Effie—"

She stared at Tod. "How can you smile at a time like this?" she demanded.

"Because I got it," he said. "Finally."

"Got what?"

"The e-pet–nappers. Remember I said there was something familiar about the note? It's the bad spelling. Mr. Brock would never misspell Shakespeare's name."

"You're right," said Tessa. "Much less use a quote like that!"

"Who are the worst spellers in the whole school? And the meanest?" asked Tod.

"Notso and Never," said Tessa. "The Gneiss twins." She shook her head, looking outraged and bewildered at the same time. "But why would they do this?"

"For fun. To make people suffer. You know how warped they are."

"Mmm," said Tessa. There was always some story going around school about the not-so-nice Gneiss twins—that they owned every vampire movie ever made, that Nancy collected voodoo dolls, even that Ned once gave his orthodontist a heart attack by wearing blood-squirting fangs to the office.

"But what about the Shakespeare quote?" she asked. "They hate Shakespeare."

"Sure, they hate Shakespeare, but they hate Mr. Brock even worse," Tod reminded her. "Brock is always quoting Shakespeare, and he's big on cruelty-free projects. Remember how he wouldn't let Ned do the thing with the butterflies? I'll bet Ned's getting revenge."

"Oh! You're right!" said Tessa. "And when Brock taught drama he wouldn't let Nancy play Captain Hook. That really got her steamed."

"They're a real grudge team," said Tod. "They get revenge, plus a bonus."

"What bonus?"

"They get to torture the e-pets."

"Aaagh! Effie!" cried Tessa. "We've got to stop them."

"We will," said Tod, holding up the Do Right. "With this."

Now Tessa smiled. "This is going to be fun," she said.

"For us," said her brother. "Not for them."

———

The Gneiss twins lived in a modest house on a quiet street not far from the school. Tod and Tessa rattled over there quickly on their bikes.

The twins were on their front lawn, poking at something in the grass with long, thin, pointy sticks, the kind from a Pick Up Sticks game. As Tod and Tessa approached, they saw that the Gneiss twins were tormenting a caterpillar.

Ned looked up. "What are you doing here?" he asked. Nancy just glared at them. They didn't even pretend to be friendly. They knew that a visit from Tod and Tessa meant some kind of trouble.

"Not much," said Tod.

"Actually, we think it's time to be friends," said Tessa loudly and clearly. "I mean, we're all twins, after all. And you guys are so cool!" She listened for Effie's beep, hoping she was somewhere nearby, waiting to be rescued.

"Spare me," said Ned, getting up. "This is private property. No dorks allowed."

"Dorks!" said Tod.

Wielding their pointy sticks, Ned and Nancy headed menacingly toward the twins. Tod backed up a little, while Tessa aimed the Do Right.

"Don't you think it's time to check on the hostages?" she asked softly.

"What hostages?" said Nancy, eyes narrowed.

"What are you talking about?" demanded Ned, holding his stick as if it were a dagger.

Tod took the Do Right from Tessa. This time she'd used suggestions, not commands, so why wasn't it working? Maybe her aim was bad. He pointed the device at Ned, then at Nancy.

"How about if you both shut up?" he said as smoothly as he could.

"How about if you both get out of here?" snarled Ned. He bent down to pick up a stone.

Tod and Tessa jumped on their bikes and pedaled away quickly. The stone flew past them, hitting the door of a passing car with a loud *ping!* The car stopped and a red-faced man rolled down the window.

"They tried to hurt us!" whined Nancy, shooting Tessa an evil smile.

"They damaged your car!" shouted Ned.

Tod and Tessa kept pedaling until they were far from the Gneiss twins' neighborhood. They stopped at the turnoff to Lou and Lulu's road, and Tod pulled out the Do Right. "How come it didn't work with them?" he said, shaking it. "You used a suggestion. Do you think the batteries are dead?"

"It's not the batteries. I just remembered something else about the Do Right," Tessa said, leaning on her handlebars. "It only works on one person at a time. Jack told us that when he gave it to us."

Tod realized Tessa was right. "Uh-oh," he said. "Notso and Never stick together like glue."

"Not always," said Tessa. "There's one place they don't go together, because they aren't allowed."

Tod grinned. "You're pretty smart for a girl," he said. "But then, you are my twin." He biked away before Tessa could hit him.

chapter 12

The next morning after third period, Tessa followed Nancy Gneiss down the second-floor hall to the girls' bathroom. She slipped inside just as Nancy closed herself in a stall. They were alone, so Tessa hurried into the stall next to Nancy's, aimed the Do Right at Nancy under the partition, and pressed the button.

"Don't you think you should check on the hostages?" she suggested quietly.

"Good idea," came Nancy's reply. The toilet flushed. Water ran in the sink, then stopped. When Nancy left the bathroom, Tessa followed her. She trailed her down to the ground floor and then out of the building, wondering where they were heading.

Nancy walked briskly across the teachers' parking lot and along the athletic field until she came to a

Dumpster near the bleachers. She raised the lid and peered inside.

Tessa heard a weak electronic twitter—e-pets in distress!—and her heart lurched. It was such a sad sound!

Nancy smiled.

What a creep that girl is, thought Tessa. She'd meant to stay hidden, but Nancy made her so angry that she jumped out from behind the bleachers with the Do Right in her hand.

"What are *you* doing here?" demanded Nancy when she saw Tessa.

"I might ask you the same thing," said Tessa, stepping closer. "Except I know."

"Know what, Hippie Girl?" taunted Nancy. "You can't prove anything. Don't even try."

"I think I will try," said Tessa. She aimed the Do Right at Nancy. "I strongly suggest that you hand the pets over to me."

Nancy's eyes changed, taking on the dull, eager-to-please shine that meant the Do Right was working. "Good idea," she said agreeably.

"I suggest that you do it now!" said Tessa, struggling to keep her voice steady.

"Great idea." Blank-faced, Nancy reached into the Dumpster and pulled out a black plastic garbage bag. A few feeble electronic beeps came from inside, as if the pets were just barely alive.

Tessa hoped furiously that Effie was all right.

As she was about to take the bag, a shout came from across the field. Even from a distance Tessa recognized the voice. She winced. Ned Gneiss came running at them, waving and yelling. "Stop, kidnapper!" he shouted. "Stop!" Watson was with him.

Nancy looked confused. Clutching the bag, she took a step back, and Tessa heard the pets beep again.

Ned was coming closer. "She's the one!" he yelled. "She did it! That Gibson girl did it!"

Beep beep!

Tessa's heart jumped when she heard Effie's signal. She grabbed for the bag, and Nancy let it go just as Ned and Watson reached them.

"Look at that evil smile!" said Ned, pointing at Tessa. He reminded her of some hammy television lawyer, acting indignant for the jury. "It's a good thing Nancy followed her," he went on. "She was just about to kill the pets! If it wasn't for Nancy, those pets would be dead. Right, sis?"

Nancy nodded innocently.

BEEP! BEEP! BEEP! commented Effie.

"That is such a lie," said Tessa.

Watson, looking troubled, took the bag from her. "I'd better bring this to the principal," he said.

Tessa stuck the Do Right in her pocket hastily, hoping nobody had noticed it. As she did, a piece of paper came out of her pocket and fluttered to the ground.

It was the copy of the note.

Nancy smiled spitefully at Tessa. "Guess you'll have some explaining to do."

"Your word against mine," retorted Tessa. At least they hadn't gotten hold of the Do Right, she thought.

chapter 13

"**A**t least they didn't get hold of the Do Right," Tod said later that day as he and Tessa walked home from school. "Can you imagine what they'd do with *that?*"

"I know," said Tessa gloomily. "But if you're trying to cheer me up, don't bother." She was in trouble. Because she'd been found with the copy of the note, Mr. Harken thought she was the petnapper. He was going to think about her punishment over the weekend, and Tessa was pretty sure he'd call Lou and Lulu also.

"So Harken didn't believe you?" asked Tod.

"Nope. Why should he? Notso and Never are really good liars, which I'm not." She kicked a stone. They were on the dirt road leading to the farm. "You know how Lulu and Lou are always talking about karma, and what goes around comes around?" she said.

Tod nodded.

"Well, how can it be true? The Gneisses do nasty stuff all the time, and they keep getting away with it. Why aren't they punished?"

"Maybe they will be," said Tod.

"Bet?" She stuck her pinkie out.

He sighed. "No."

"See?" said Tessa. It was so unfair. How could anybody believe Ned and Nancy instead of her? They were such conniving liars! Effie had practically beeped her head off in the principal's office!

Tessa patted the little e-pet. "At least you're safe," she said.

Effie smiled.

chapter 14

"**H**ow's everything at school?" asked Lulu after Lou had said grace.

"Okay," said Tessa.

"Just okay?"

The twins looked at each other. Were they ready to tell their grandparents about Effie? Maybe. Maybe not. Were they ready to complain about the Gneiss twins? Definitely.

"You'll never believe what happened," said Tessa.

"Try us," said Lulu, dishing out the chili.

A few miles away the Gneiss twins were eating dinner with their mother. Mr. Gneiss wouldn't be home until much later. His shish kebab restaurant, the Silver Skewer, kept him busy until ten or eleven every night.

"How is everything at school?" asked Mrs. Gneiss.

"Fine," said Ned, stabbing a potato with his fork.

Nancy used her knife to push four peas, slowly and deliberately, onto the tines of her fork.

"We helped recover a bunch of stolen stuff . . . ," began Nancy.

". . . and the principal thanked us. Personally," said Ned. "It was pretty cool." He speared a piece of lamb with his knife.

"Use your fork, Ned," said Mrs. Gneiss. "What was stolen?" she asked.

They gave her a bland look. "Some toys," they said.

"One at a time," said Mrs. Gneiss. She didn't like it when they spoke together. Sometimes she could swear they did it on purpose.

"Electronic pets," said Ned.

"We already told you," Nancy said. "You have to feed them and play with them and rest them . . ."

"Or they die," said Ned. "They get weaker and weaker, and they make little beeping noises. *Eeeep . . . eeeep*," he squeaked feebly, fluttering his eyelids and rocking back and forth in his chair.

"It's *so* sad," agreed Nancy, smiling at Ned's antics.

Ned grinned at his mother's look of alarm. "Just teasing, Mom," he said.

I wish I had normal children, thought Mrs. Gneiss. She put down her fork, realizing that she was no longer hungry. She would talk to her husband that night, she decided. No matter how late he came home.

"And that's the whole story," said Tessa, finishing the saga of the petnapping. She'd managed to leave out the Do Right. She'd also failed to mention the reason for Effie's beeping, though she had told her grandparents that Effie came from Jack's shop.

Beep beep, said Effie. Tessa ignored her. "It just wasn't fair," she said. "First they stole them, then they pretended to find them."

"And blamed us," added Tod. "Actually, more Tessa."

"Then they got rewarded for stealing and lying," said Tessa. "Which totally sucks," she added under her breath.

Lulu looked at her sharply. "Life isn't always fair in the short run," she said. "But what goes around comes around."

"Things work out in the long run," said Lou.

"You have to do the right thing, even if you don't get credit for it," said Lulu.

"Whatever," said Tod. Sometimes his grandparents seemed really naive to him. But then they'd been out of middle school for a long time.

"That's what I told your principal," said Lou.

"He called?" Tessa's heart thumped.

"This afternoon."

"Seconds?" asked Lulu.

"With pleasure." Lou held out his plate for another slice of strawberry rhubarb pie. "Anyway," he went on, "he told me about the pets, and how you swore you hadn't stolen them, but you had the note in your pocket." Lou took a bite of pie.

"He said he thought you were lying. I told him you were truthful to a fault. I also said that no matter how things looked, I was sure you'd done the right thing."

Lou peered at Tessa over his spectacles. "Which you did, didn't you?"

Tessa searched her conscience. She had been hiding some of the truth, she knew that. But compared to Ned and Nancy, she and Tod were saints.

She nodded.

"I thought so," said Lou.

"Me too," said Lulu. "No matter how much time your parents put into their business, and no matter how caught up in it they get, Lou and I know they've always taken the time to raise you right."

"Thanks," mumbled Tessa gratefully. "You guys are the best."

Tod glanced at the clock. "It's late," he said. "Six-forty."

"Late for what?" asked Lou.

"We have to return Effie and the, uh—" Tod stopped himself.

"And the what?" asked Lou through a mouthful of pie.

"Oh, nothing," said Tod. He didn't want to tell his grandparents about the Do Right. They'd never understand. "And just look around the mall."

Beep beep. Effie's little mouth smiled and wobbled up and down.

"Funny little thing," said Lou. "Can I see it?"

Tessa passed Effie over to him. "What does it do?" Lou asked.

"Not a whole lot," said Tod.

Beep beep!

"Color reminds me of Jimi Hendrix's guitar," said Lou. "Same bright pink." He handed Effie back to

Tessa. "Did I ever tell you about the time I jammed with Jimi at Woodstock?"

"Yup," said Tod. "Lots of times."

"It was fantastic," said Lou. "Three, maybe four hours just flew by."

Beep beep, said Effie.

"I'm pretty sure he was going to ask me to join the band—"

Beep beep! said Effie.

"My, that thing is noisy," commented Lulu. Then she said, "Lou, let the kids go. They're in a hurry. Tod, Tessa, go straight to the mall and when you get there, don't dawdle. Come straight back, you hear?"

"We will," said Tessa, grabbing her pack and heading out the door.

Beep beep, said Effie.

chapter 15

The twins pedaled furiously across the parking lot and jumped off their bikes at the mall entrance. "We're late," panted Tessa.

"That's okay," said Tod. "Jack can adjust time for us again. And if that doesn't prove he's an alien, I'd like to know what does," he added.

Tessa still wasn't convinced. "He owns a store," she said. "Why can't he just keep it open?" She headed for the escalator. "That whole Back thing is so bizarre."

"Not really," said Tod. "Grown-ups are always adjusting time. They set it forward and back a whole hour for daylight savings. What's so different about Jack adjusting it for a few minutes?"

"Nothing, I guess." Tessa knew that Tod was being perfectly logical. She also knew there had to be a big difference between human adults adjusting time for the whole planet and somebody who might be an alien adjusting time for a pair of almost-ten-year-old twins.

"He'll have to do it again," she said, pointing at the big clock inside the entrance. It read 7:01.

They took the escalator two steps at a time. Nobody else was on it, so they could run as fast as they liked. It was almost like flying. They were on Level 3 in seconds.

They started walking backward, searching the store windows for a red reflection.

It was 7:03 when Tessa saw the sign:

GEMINI JACK'S U RENT ALL
Be First in the Universe!

It blinked on, then off, in the Home Office Depot window.

Tessa punched Tod in the side and he saw it too.

"Great," he said. They turned, and there was the dusty little corridor with Jack's store at the end of it.

Jack was inside, leaning on the counter. There was a bright square of light on the wall opposite him, and in the square was a woman wearing a long, silvery skirt.

Tessa pulled on the door. It was locked. The woman turned and stared at Tessa. Tessa stared back. The woman looked just like Jack—except for her expression, which was stern and serious.

"Jack?" called Tod, knocking.

Jack looked up, alarmed. He saw Tessa, reached under the counter . . . and Tessa found herself walking up to the door and turning the knob.

This time when the door bonged Jack was alone.

"Hello," he said cheerfully.

"What happened just then?" asked Tessa.

"You were late, so I pressed Back," said Jack. "Same as before. It's risky to do it too often, you know. If you keep folding time back, it will tear, just like paper."

"I didn't mean that," said Tessa. "I—I thought I saw somebody else in here."

I know I did, thought Tod.

Jack shrugged and smiled a thin little smile. "Must have been your imagination," he said.

Beep beep, said Effie from inside Tessa's pack.

"Ah! FM is back," said Jack, changing the subject. "So your rescue operation was a success. Wonderful. Tell me about it."

"You'll never believe what happened," said Tessa, placing Effie and the Do Right on the counter.

"Really," said Tod.

"Try me," said Jack.

"So how come you were out at the Dumpster with Hippie Girl?" Ned asked Nancy. "That wasn't part of the plan." He came into her room, kicking the door shut behind him.

Nancy was painting her toenails. "No clue," she muttered. "I was in the girls' bathroom. The next thing I knew, I was at the Dumpster, and she was with me. It was like a bad dream."

"We almost got caught," Ned complained.

One of Nancy's eyebrows went up. "But we didn't." She closed the bottle of polish and examined her toenails. They were the color of dried blood.

"We might have," said Ned. "Besides, the whole plan is a flop. We didn't get even with Brock," he whined, his fists clenching, "and we didn't get to torture any e-pets."

"I know," said Nancy. "Too bad about that. On the other hand, we did get the Dork twins in trouble."

"Only one of them," grumbled Ned.

"We'll kill her e-pet next," Nancy promised.

"When? How? Tell me!"

"Calm down, Neddy," said Nancy. "Here's my plan. . . ."

"The worst part," said Tessa as she and Tod finished telling Jack about the Gneiss twins, "is that they blamed me for everything—and got away with it."

"Wonderful," said Jack.

"Wonderful?"

"I mean terrible," said Jack. "You are sure they're twins?"

"Fraternal, like us," said Tod.

"They give twins a bad name," said Tessa. "They lie, they steal, they cheat. . . ."

"They sound ruthless. Are they ruthless?" asked Jack.

"Sure," said Tessa, thinking of the e-pets in the Dumpster. "Very."

"Aggressive?"

"Yes."

"Vengeful?"

"They definitely hold grudges," said Tod.

Jack leaned forward, his black eyes bright with

interest. "Would you say they had criminal tendencies?"

Tessa stared at Jack. "You sound as if you know them," she said.

"No," said Jack. His smooth, pale face seemed to shine for an instant. "But I would like to."

Now even Tod looked surprised. "Why?" he asked.

"I'm doing research on human units—I mean twins," said Jack. "Good ones, bad ones, very bad ones . . ."

"The Gneiss twins are the worst," said Tessa.

"Do you really think so?" asked Jack hopefully. "I would like to be first in the universe to know for certain."

The twins nodded, puzzled. Tod wondered again what Jack was really up to. Maybe he did have a hidden agenda. Then Tod saw Jack's expression change, as if he'd heard a signal, or an alarm.

"Ah!" exclaimed Jack, hurrying out from behind the counter. "It's late and I must close the shop."

"But—" Tessa's eyes went to the counter. "Can I say goodbye to Effie?" she asked.

"You don't have to say goodbye to her," said Jack. "Take her home. Just bring her back tomorrow. There's no school tomorrow, isn't that correct?"

"Right—it's Saturday," said Tessa. She scooped Effie up happily.

"What time do you open?" asked Tod as Jack whisked them out the door.

"Ten." The door shut behind them and the shop window went dark instantly.

The twins stood in the hallway. Tod shook his head. He hardly knew what to think.

"You're right about one thing," said Tessa as they walked to the escalator.

"What?"

"He's definitely an alien."

"What changed your mind?" asked Tod.

"Anybody who wants to meet the Gneiss twins has to be from another planet."

"I've found them," Jack reported to his twin. "I'm sure of it." He was so excited that he started to glow.

"Have you tested them?" she asked.

"Tomorrow."

"Have you met them?"

"Tomorrow."

Jill frowned. "Who are they?"

"According to my first unit, they are wily, ruthless, and aggressive. They are also extremely vengeful. They sound perfect."

"How do you plan to make contact?" asked Jill.

"I am nearly one hundred percent certain that they will follow my first unit here in an effort to get even with them."

Jill made an exasperated noise.

"My first unit is very reliable," protested Jack. "And I have a very strong feeling about this."

"I hope you are right," said Jill. "Observe the unit carefully. You know what to look for. Repeated unprovoked aggressive behavior against humans. Indifference to distress signals from helpless animals. Rudeness. Petty cruelty. Violent impulses."

Jack nodded.

"The final test is the gene tracker," she said. "Should I beam it to the store?"

"Send it to the mall," said Jack. "That way they'll test themselves."

"Even better," she said. She started to fade. "Jack?"

"Yes?"

"This is our last chance. If they don't come through . . ." She sighed. "Just keep your fingers crossed."

"All sixteen of them," said Jack as she disappeared.

chapter 16

*L*ate that night, Mr. and Mrs. Gneiss sat in their kitchen drinking tea.

"Georgeu, I'm afraid," said Mrs. Gneiss. There were lines of worry on her forehead and circles under her eyes.

"Mirjana," said her husband, "we're Americans now. Our families have been in this country for seventy-five years. Those old Romanian stories are nothing but folktales. Superstition."

"But what if they're true?" demanded Mrs. Gneiss. "The signs are starting to show. You've seen them yourself."

"What? The lamb on the skewers? The jelly beans on the toothpicks?" said her husband. "That has nothing—nothing—to do with Vlad. It's kid stuff. Harmless."

"It's—not just hot dogs on sticks," she said. "It's other things too. Live things."

Her husband's dark eyes widened. "Really?"

She nodded. "Butterflies. Worms. I found them with a frog last week. I stopped them just in time." She shuddered. "They are twins of the thirteenth generation, Georgeu, and they will soon be ten years old. The legend says that the blood of the Impaler emerges in just such children—"

"I know what the legend says, and I don't believe it!" he said, his voice rising. "The twins are not modern-day monsters, no matter how much they like wienie roasts!"

"Shhh!" warned his wife. "They'll hear you!"

"They're asleep," said Mr. Gneiss. "They haven't heard a thing."

But he was wrong.

"Have you ever had the feeling you were being followed?" Tessa asked Tod.

"Now?" he asked, and she nodded.

Tod looked around. The mall was pretty quiet for a Saturday morning. There were a few people near the wishing well in the atrium, admiring a gleaming new kiosk that looked like a cash machine. A man put some quarters in it. Nothing suspicious about that.

Other shoppers strolled by—parents with young children, middle-aged couples, women shopping in twos or threes—all looking perfectly normal. "It's your imagination," Tod told Tessa.

"That's what you always say," she retorted. Then they were on Level 3, looking for Jack's again. Tessa turned on her heel, took her brother's hand, and took a backward step. Tod joined in as smoothly as if they were dancing.

One step. Two steps. And there it was:

GEMINI JACK'S U RENT ALL
Be First in the Universe!

They walked down the narrow corridor toward the blinking red sign and opened the door. It bonged.

"Hello and thank you," said Jack in greeting.

"Thank you for what?" asked the twins.

"For bringing the twins. Ned and Nancy. I am looking forward to meeting them."

"We didn't bring them," said Tod.

"Still, they are on their way," said Jack, whose face seemed to be pulsing with light. His black eyes flashed. "They should be here in just under a minute."

"How do you know?" asked Tod.

Jack held up a little triangular mirror. "This shows the future—the very near future," he said. "They just got off the escalator." The twins saw a small, very clear image of Ned and Nancy, standing in the corridor in front of Home Office Depot.

"So we *were* being followed," Tessa said to Tod. "I knew it!"

"I knew it too," said Tod.

Beep beep! said Effie from Tessa's palm.

"Ah, there she is!" exclaimed Jack when he saw Effie. "Just put her on the counter, please. And then I have a favor to ask."

"Sure," said Tessa. "What is it?"

"I would like to meet the Gneiss twins alone—or rather, with FM. Effie. So it is necessary for you to disappear."

"You want us to leave?" asked Tod.

Jack went behind the counter. "No. Disappear." He reached under the counter and gave them each a pair of dark wraparound sunglasses. "If you put these on, you will not be visible. Would you mind doing that? Quickly?"

The glasses were so light they were almost weightless, and the lenses were a dark silvery gray. But when Tessa put them on everything looked exactly the same, as if the lenses were clear.

"I thought these were sunglasses," she said. "Nothing's any darker."

"You look a lot different," said Tod.

"How? And why are you staring at the floor?"

"Because that's all I can see of you—a shadow."

"Put yours on," said Tessa. When he put the glasses on, he disappeared. But when she looked at the floor, Tessa could see his shadow.

"Wow!" she said. "Touch your nose."

"Okay." The shadow on the floor touched its nose.

"Holy moly!" exclaimed Tessa.

"If you keep them on, the Gneiss twins will not see you," said Jack.

"Really?" asked Tod.

"Cool!" said Tessa. She had always dreamed of being invisible, and the thought of watching Ned and Nancy without being seen was thrilling. "What's this all about?" she asked. "What are you going to do to them?"

For a moment Jack was silent. Then he said, "I am not free to tell you at this time. But you have my word that no harm will come to them. Absolutely none."

Bummer! thought Tessa, and then felt a twinge of guilt.

Too bad, thought Tod.

"And please remain silent," added Jack.

The door bonged and the Gneiss twins came in.

chapter 17

"**H**ello," said Jack. "May I help you?"

Ned and Nancy looked around the shop quickly, seeming surprised that they were the only customers. "I could *swear* they were in here," Ned hissed to Nancy. Tod and Tessa smiled. The Gneiss twins really couldn't see them.

"We were with some friends," Nancy told Jack. "And we lost them. I thought they came in here."

Beep beep, said Effie, who was sitting on the counter.

"A boy and a girl your age?" said Jack, his black eyes intent on them. "They just left."

Beep beep, said Effie again.

Nancy started when she heard the e-pet. "What's that stup—I mean, what's that noise?" she asked Jack. Then she spotted Effie. "Oh, it's one of those electronic pets." She gave Jack a sugary, bright-eyed smile. "I *love* them," she said.

You liar! thought Tessa.

Beep beep! said Effie.

"Were you looking for anything special today?" asked Jack. Without seeming to, he had arranged some new merchandise on the counter. Now Effie was surrounded by half a dozen odd little gadgets—including something that looked just like the Do Right. Tessa gulped. What was Jack up to?

"Not really," said Ned. "Unless you've got any poison darts to sell us."

"Neddy!" gasped Nancy in mock horror. "He's only joking," she told Jack.

Beep beep, said Effie. Nancy's face twitched with dislike at the sound, but Jack ignored it. "Excuse me," he said, moving to the door marked PRIVATE at the end of the counter. "I have to make a call. Feel free to look around."

Smiling affably, he walked through the door—holding a pair of sunglasses exactly like the ones he had given to Tod and Tessa. Tessa realized that Jack was going to disappear too.

Without making a sound, a shadowy, transparent Jack came back through the door wearing the sun-glasses and stationed himself behind the counter, next to Tessa and Tod. He held up eleven or twelve fingers to his mouth, signaling them to be quiet. Tessa and Tod could see him, but Ned and Nancy couldn't.

They really don't know we're here, thought Tod. Incredible.

What will those horrible creeps do, now that they think they're alone? wondered Tessa, itching with curiosity.

The instant Jack was gone Nancy picked up Effie. "Look at this," she said. "It's just like the one that belonged to Hippie Girl."

Ned grabbed Effie. "Since you hate these so much, let's think of a really great way to finish this one off."

Tessa nearly cried out but stopped herself just in time.

Nancy grabbed Effie back. "What if that weird guy misses it?" She looked at the e-pet closely. "Huh. It is the exact one," she said. "I wonder what it's doing here."

Ned shrugged. "Maybe the Dork twins had it with them and forgot it."

Dork twins! thought Tod and Tessa.

"Anyway, who cares?" continued Ned. "Just take it. That weird guy won't notice."

"See anything you like?" asked Jack, appearing so suddenly that Nancy gave a little shriek of surprise and dropped Effie on the counter.

"Whoa!" said Ned, startled. "Didn't see you there."

"Nothing you'd like to take away with you?" Jack's voice was soft, but his smile was cold. "Your friend left that little pink device," he said. "Would you mind returning it to her?"

"Noooo!" Tessa moaned softly.

"Glad to!" Nancy exclaimed loudly at the very same moment. She grabbed Effie and hurried to the door. "We'll make sure she gets it!"

Then she and Ned bolted out of the store so fast that Tessa could hardly hear Effie's parting beep. The instant the door bonged Tessa whipped off her glasses. Her face was flushed and her curly red hair frizzed out around her face the way it did when she was agitated.

"Jack! What is going on?" she cried. "Why did you let them take Effie?"

Jack's face was bright, almost joyful. "I will tell you later," he said. "There is no time now. We must follow and observe. You are twins—will you help me, please? Put on your glasses. Hurry!"

"Effie won't get hurt, will she?" asked Tessa. She'd

always wished she could be invisible, but now that it was happening, she was completely shaken. Who knew what Nancy might do to Effie?

"Nobody will get hurt," promised Jack. "Now, let's go. We can't let them out of our sight."

The strangeness of the situation hit Tod like a sockful of wet sand and he froze. Was he really about to follow an alien and chase the two meanest kids in school through the mall? It was all so freaky that for a moment he simply couldn't move.

He stood there, thinking of the way Lou liked to say "You've got to go with the changes" when something surprising or unpleasant happened. It was one of Lou's favorite sayings, and now Tod finally understood it.

He went.

chapter 18

They caught up with the Gneiss twins on Level 3. A DANGER! WET FLOOR! sign blocked their way, and Ned kicked it aside without stopping. Skirting the puddle, they came to Gourmet Gallery. Nancy grabbed a lollipop from a baby in a stroller whose mother's attention was on the window. The baby shrieked. Its mother spun around, alarmed. Nancy strode along with Ned, the lollipop in her mouth.

"Do you see the Dork twins anywhere?" Ned asked her.

"Nuh-uh. But it doesn't matter now—I have her precious pet. Oooh, look." Nancy pointed at a display in Natureland's window. "Beetles on pins. I *love* those!"

Ned glanced inside. "Whoa. Live turtles. Those

are fun." Nancy followed him into the store. A man was paying for something at the cash register, and a couple was gazing into the tropical fish tanks along the wall. Otherwise, the store was empty.

Or so it seemed. Three shadows slipped through the door right after the Gneiss twins.

Ned and Nancy strolled past a terrarium, where half a dozen sleepy-looking turtles basked on the rocks. Ned looked around to make sure nobody was watching, then flipped the turtles over one by one. Their heads disappeared into their shells, but their arms and legs flailed as if signaling for help.

Now Ned held a Swiss Army knife and was pulling out a curly metal thing that Tod recognized as a corkscrew. Its tip glinted, pointy and sharp.

Tod's stomach clenched. Ned smiled.

"Remember all that stuff Mom and Dad were talking about last night? The stuff about us being the thirteenth in line, and how we've inherited something Mom's scared of?"

Nancy nodded, her eyes bright.

"Well, Dad doesn't think it's true, but I think it is. And I can prove it. Watch this," Ned said, closing in on the biggest of the turtles.

Tessa almost screamed. This was too gross! How could Jack stand there so calmly? Ned had to be stopped! Before he could stab the turtle, she swiped at a row of boxes on a nearby shelf and they thudded to the floor. The couple at the fish tanks turned to look at Ned and Nancy. They froze.

"Who did that?" whispered Ned. His hands were in his pockets and the knife had disappeared.

"Don't look at me," snapped Nancy.

"Hey! What's going on over there?" called the clerk. His customers were staring at Ned and Nancy, frowning.

"Whoops! Sorry!" Nancy hit just the right apologetic note. "We'll pick them up, no problem," she called, reshelving the boxes hastily before she and Ned made a quick exit.

Tod and Tessa flipped the turtles over and hurried after Jack, who was right behind the Gneiss twins. They were walking toward the food court.

"You must not interfere," Jack told Tessa as they followed.

"You can't let them *kill* things!" she protested.

"That was pretty disgusting," said Tod. "Even for them."

"Speak quietly, please," whispered Jack. "You are not visible, but you must not draw attention to yourselves." They moved along in silence for a moment, passing an elderly couple holding hands.

"I did say nobody would get hurt," Jack reminded the twins softly.

"Promise?" insisted Tessa. She was still worried about Effie. There was probably even more to worry about, she thought, even if she didn't know exactly what it was.

"Yes."

They were nearing the food court, a circular atrium ringed by carts selling sandwiches, soft drinks, frozen yogurt, and coffee. There was usually music playing in this part of the mall, but today something unusual was happening. As they approached, Tessa heard the sound of a man's voice coming over a microphone, and some scattered laughter.

The voice sounded familiar, thought Tessa. Then she saw why.

Watson, dressed in jeans and a T-shirt, was talking to the people in the food court. A sign on an easel said:

START YOUR DAY WITH A SMILE!
MEET COMIC JAMES WATSON TODAY AT 10:30!

There were about six people seated at the little tables, drinking coffee out of paper cups. They were listening to Watson, smiling, as he finished a joke.

"Clerk says, 'The kind that waddle, or the kind you eat with cweem cheese?'

"Man says, 'Are you making fun of me?'

"Clerk says, 'What do you think I am, cwazy?' "

The people laughed and Watson beamed. Tessa noticed that his hands were shaking. She wondered if this was the first time he had ever done his act for grown-ups.

"You're a great audience, you know that?" said Watson. "No! You really are. Which reminds me, did you hear the one about the mushroom?" He twirled the microphone cord nervously. "Got invited to all the parties—"

"—because he was such a fungi! Fun guy, get it? Yuk, yuk!" The voice, heavy with sarcasm, belonged to Ned Gneiss. He and Nancy were concealed behind a pillar, sneering.

Watson, a little shaken, smiled uncertainly. There was an uncomfortable silence. "That's right," he said quietly. "Fun guy."

Then he tried again. "You're a great audience, so

here's another question for you, and this one's a little harder." He paused. "How do you get a handkerchief to dance? You—"

"You put a little boogie in it," called Ned. "That joke's an antique, dude!"

"I heard it in kindergarten!" added Nancy, her voice dripping contempt.

A man folded his paper and stood. So did a grayhaired woman carrying a little dog, and a bespectacled man in a turban. Half the tiny audience drifted away.

Watson's face crumpled, and Tessa felt a wave of pity for him. But Jack? His shadow was nodding enthusiastically.

"Excellent," he whispered. "Excellent!"

"Excellent? Blecch! That's so *mean!*" said Tessa.

Tod's shadow nodded vehemently in agreement. Watson looked at his watch, then out at the empty tables where the audience had been. Moving slowly, he began to pack up his sound system. He looked as if he'd shrunk.

"Poor guy," murmured Tessa.

"Shhh!" said Jack. "Where are the Gneiss twins? I don't see them."

Tod's shadow pointed. Ned and Nancy were getting on the down escalator.

"Hurry," whispered Jack. "We are almost finished."

Good! thought the twins. But finished with what?

chapter *19*

Ned and Nancy were on the main floor, looking at the new kiosk near the wishing well. Its big red LED sign said:

ANCESTOR TRACKER!
SEARCH THE PAST!
FIND YOUR FAMILY!
Three generations, 25 cents!

"Here's our chance to find out if it's true," said Nancy.

"If what's true?"

"You know, what Dad was saying last night. About Vlad and the thirteenth generation."

Vlad? thought Tod and Tessa. Who's that?

"Whoa! Good idea," said Ned, digging some change out of his pocket.

"Any quarters?" asked Nancy.

"No, but that's easy." He reached down into the wishing well and grabbed some quarters.

"Good, good," said Jack very softly.

Good? thought Tessa. That money was supposed to go to the animal shelter! Her opinion of Jack was changing for the worse.

"How many generations?" asked Ned, feeding three quarters into the machine. "Wasn't Vlad back in the Middle Ages or something?"

"Try twelve," said Nancy. The machine lit up, and Ned went through the opening screens. "Go to Romania," she instructed him. "And remember, our name used to be different—like Gniescu or something."

"Oh, right," said Ned. "Dad said the immigration guys at Ellis Island changed it." He put another quarter in the machine and went to a list of long, complicated-looking names. He clicked. The screen changed and changed again. The listings were getting shorter.

"One more and we'll be in the fifteenth century," said Ned.

Tessa read the names on the screen. There were some strange but easy ones like Bodo and Platzik, and some that were so complicated she couldn't imagine how to pronounce them. She guessed they were Romanian—she wasn't sure. And she had no idea who the Gneiss twins were looking for. A Romanian from the fifteenth century called Vlad? Who was *that*?

Wow, thought Tod. Cool machine.

Nancy fished another quarter from the well and gave it to Ned. Once more the screen changed, and now the Gneiss twins let out an eerie howl of delight that raised goose bumps on Tessa's arms.

"It's true! It's true!" they cried, slapping palms. "Do we have great ancestors or *what*?"

Tessa, sensing Tod and Jack on either side of her, read the screen. It said: "Vlad Tepes, called Vlad the Impaler (1420–1477), was the real-life inspiration for the legendary Count Dracula." Stifling an exclamation, she staggered backward on wobbly legs until she felt a wall behind her.

"Dracula! I can't believe it!" whispered Tod.

I can, thought Tessa.

"I can't either!" Soft as it was, Jack's voice throbbed with happiness. "Dracula was evil, almost a monster, was he not?"

The twins managed to nod.

"What news!" Jack said happily. "I must inform my sister! She will be so pleased!" His shadow flickered away.

"Wait! Where are you going?" said Tessa.

"To the store! And I must hurry."

"But you said you'd explain—" She tried to keep her voice down, but a few heads turned as she called out to Jack.

"Later!" He was gone.

Ned and Nancy didn't even glance in Tessa's direction. "No wonder those turtles looked so appealing. Wish we still had them," said Ned, pulling out his Swiss Army knife and opening the corkscrew. "We could celebrate."

"Excuse me," said a teenage girl holding on to a little boy by his overall strap, "do you have the time?"

"Of course," said Nancy sweetly. She pretended to check her watch. "It's twelve-fifteen."

Beep beep! said Effie. She was in Nancy's pocket, but Tessa could hear her.

"Ohmygod! We're late!" cried the girl.

Then Ned pretended to check his watch. "Whoa, sis," he said, "I think your watch is wrong. Mine says it's much later—twelve-thirty."

Beep beep! said Effie again. The girl moaned and the little boy broke away from her, charging for the escalator. "Henry! Henry! Come back here!" The girl's voice was frantic. "We have to go *right now!*"

"What were you saying about celebrating?" said Nancy, watching the girl race after the little boy.

"Be nice to have a real victim," said Ned with an evil grin.

"We do." She pulled Effie out of her pocket. Tessa went cold with panic.

"Whoa! Great idea!" said Ned. "Hold her steady."

No! thought Tessa. Her heart was doing a drumroll.

Ned placed the corkscrew's pointy tip right on Effie's face and pressed. "She's plastic," he grunted. "Kinda hard."

"Then push harder," said Nancy sweetly.

"Stop!" Tessa screamed. Tod grabbed her arm to restrain her. "Shhh!" he whispered as the Gneiss twins, startled, looked around. They couldn't see who was shouting at them, though, because Tessa was still invisible.

"Cool it, Tessa," whispered Tod. Instead, she ran right up to them, yelling, "Stop that right now! Leave her alone!" At the same time, she pulled off her sunglasses so that she appeared right in front of them, screaming and a little wild-eyed.

"You!" said Nancy hoarsely. Her eyes rolled back in her head and her knees buckled. She fell, dropping Effie, to lie flat on the floor with her sneakers pointing straight up into the air.

She even faints neatly, thought Tessa.

Ned didn't say anything. He had already hit the floor.

"Put your glasses back on!" Tod, still a shadow, hovered nearby. "Maybe we can get away." There weren't many people around, only an elderly woman wearing a baseball cap and carrying a cane.

But it was too late. Tessa grabbed Effie, and then Watson was at her side, back in his guard's uniform. "Where'd this machine come from?" he asked. Then he saw the twins. "And what happened to them?" Ned and Nancy were as still as mannequins.

Tessa made a flicking "Get out of here" gesture to Tod, who floated off in the direction of the escalator. The elderly woman was coming their way.

"Uh, I can explain," Tessa told Watson, who was kneeling with his face inches from Ned's.

"Well, they're breathing," said Watson. "What'd you do, slug them?" Even now he couldn't resist an attempt at a joke.

"They fainted," said Tessa. "I guess they weren't too happy to see me."

He laughed. "I guess not."

"I liked your act," said Tessa.

Beep beep, said Effie before Tessa shoved her deep in a pocket.

"You did?" Watson looked really pleased, and she was tempted to tell him that the Gneiss twins, descendants of Vlad the Impaler, better known as Count Dracula, were the ones who had ruined his comedy debut.

"Excuse me, young man." The old woman had bright blue eyes and was smaller than Tessa. "I was watching. I saw everything."

"Yes?" Watson turned his attention to her, and at that moment the Gneiss twins rose into the air, shimmering, and then dispersed like an old-fashioned cartoon explosion. They were gone, soundlessly and completely, in a breath.

Nobody saw but Tessa and the old woman.

"Yes?" Watson repeated, leaning politely toward the woman. Tessa could tell that the old woman was trying to speak. She was blinking hard and moving her mouth, but no sound came out. She lifted her cane and pointed with it to the place where the twins had been.

Watson turned. "Well, look at that," he said. "They're gone. Guess they're okay."

"They . . . they . . . !" Another second and the woman might actually tell Watson what she'd seen. Watson probably wouldn't believe her, but Tessa decided not to wait.

"Whoops! I forgot!" she said. "I have to meet my brother."

She ran.

chapter 20

"Tod? Tod!" Tessa ran up the escalator, calling her brother's name. She got some surprised looks from the shoppers she passed, but trying to explain that she was chasing somebody invisible would have been a waste of time, so she kept going.

"Tod!" She was on Level 3 now, right behind a big, gliding shadow. "Take off your glasses!" she whispered. Fortunately, nobody was around.

"No way!" It *was* Tod. "Jack told us not to take them off, remember? Not that you paid any attention. He'll never lend us any cool stuff again."

"Well, what was I supposed to do," said Tessa, "let those little vampires impale Effie?" She wished her brother would become visible. It was hard to argue with a shadow. "Would you *please* take them off?" she asked. "There's nobody up here but us."

"Okay, okay." Tod took off the glasses, appearing so suddenly that Tessa jumped back, even though she was expecting to see him. It must have been really scary when she appeared in front of Ned and Nancy, she thought, feeling a thrill of satisfaction.

"Satisfied?" said Tod. "I like being invisible much better," he grumbled.

"Fine," said Tessa, "but listen. Notso and Never? They disappeared!"

Tod put the glasses back on. "Good," he said, shadowy again.

"Tod! Don't *do* that!" exclaimed Tessa.

"I like being invisible," his voice whispered from nearby.

She groped around for his arm, but he slid away. "Tod, listen! They *really* disappeared," she said. "They sparkled and dematerialized, just like they were in a science fiction movie! It was spooky."

"Good riddance," said Tod. "Did anybody see?"

"Just me and this old lady. Watson was there, but he missed it."

"That sounds right," said Tod. He glided ahead of her and turned so that they could link arms. "Let's go to the store. I bet Jack knows what happened."

Tessa wondered whether their usual routine would work if Tod was just a shadow. But it did.

They took three steps backward and saw the sign:

GEMINI JACK'S U RENT ALL
Be First in the Universe!

It blinked on, then off. They hurried to the store, expecting to see the sign again. But they didn't. Oddly, it had stopped flashing.

The door bonged as Tessa followed Tod's shadow inside. Jack stood at the window as if he were waiting for them. The sign, Tessa saw, was gone.

"Ah!" said Jack. "I am glad you got here in time. I was afraid I wouldn't get a chance to say goodbye."

"Goodbye?"

"Yes, and please give me the glasses," said Jack to Tod's shadow. The glasses appeared in his hand and Tod sprang into visibility.

"But—where are you going?" Tod asked Jack.

"Home," said Jack. "We got what we came for."

"We?" said Tessa.

Jack looked at them with bright intensity. "You are good twins, just as we are. I recognized that quickly. So I know you can keep a secret."

They nodded. They'd been keeping a lot of them

lately. "You did say you'd explain," Tessa reminded him.

Jack pressed a row of indentations in the counter. The shop door locked. The window went dark. A square of iridescent light appeared on the wall. "Meet my twin sister, ***, I mean Jill," said Jack as a holographic image took shape.

Someone who looked very much like Jack raised her hand in greeting. She was wearing a long, silvery skirt and a serious expression, but her eyes were friendly.

"Hello!" she said. "And thank you, on behalf of the twin planets Gemini."

"What did we do?" asked Tod.

"You helped us in our search," said Jill. "As Jack said, we got what we came for." Turning slightly, she revealed a circle of brilliant blue—a porthole into space. The twins could see a blue-green planet floating there, and the familiar outline of the USA.

"Holy moly! That's the earth!" Tessa was nearly choking with excitement. "I can see Florida! Where are you?" she gasped.

Jill smiled. "I am in orbit around your planet. As soon as Jack beams himself up, we'll finish and be on our way."

"Finish what?" the twins asked together.

Jill shifted again, and now the twins could see two familiar shapes lying side by side on a metallic platform. Their eyes were closed, and tubes were coming out of their arms.

chapter 21

"*N*ed and Nancy?" said Tod.

"What are you doing to them?" asked Tessa, fascinated, scared, and excited all at once.

"Taking DNA samples," said Jill.

"From the Gneiss twins?"

"We needed samples from Earth twins," said Jill. "Highly aggressive ones. We sought that rare, virulent strain that appears, causes widespread pain and destruction, and then fades away. The kind that appeared in Genghis. And Attila." Jill smiled. "Your friends—"

Not our friends! thought the twins.

"—carry it. We consider ourselves very lucky to have found them," said Jill. "Our earlier searches proved fruitless, and our planet is in danger. There is a time constraint also. . . ."

"Earlier searches!" said Tod. "You mean you've come before?"

"Of course," Jack and Jill replied.

Tessa was dizzy with curiosity. Phrases like *alien abductions*, *UFO sightings*, and *close encounters* whirled in her brain.

"At any rate," Jill went on, "we're very grateful that you led us to the Gneiss twins. They suit our needs perfectly. And they were especially easy to transport in an unconscious state," she added to Tessa.

Tessa gulped. "I—I'm glad," she said.

Jack beamed at them. "At first I thought you might be the ones," he said.

"Really!" said Tod. He'd often felt mean enough to throw things. And he'd smoked a cigar once.

"But you failed the first test," said Jack. "You brought Effie back unharmed."

"So Ned and Nancy made the cut," said Tod, with just a touch of envy. "Are you taking them with you?" he added hopefully.

"We don't have to," said Jack. "Besides, their parents would miss them."

Tod wondered about that.

"Maybe not so much," said Tessa, who would

often say things that Tod only thought. She tried to sound persuasive.

"We don't like to interfere in the affairs of lesser, I mean other planets," said Jill. "We will beam the Gneiss twins down very soon."

"They won't remember what happened today," added Jack. "And they won't miss what we took from them."

Jill raised her hand in farewell. Her image started to fade.

"But—why the mall?" Tessa asked hastily. She had so many questions!

"Malls are fun," said Jack.

"And that's where you find really evil people," said Jill. Then she disappeared.

Late Sunday night, Mr. and Mrs. Gneiss sat in their kitchen drinking tea. The twins had said good night at nine. Going to sleep so early was unusual for Ned and Nancy. They had done many unusual things that day, and at last Mr. and Mrs. Gneiss could discuss them in private.

"I still can't believe it," said Mrs. Gneiss, turning her teacup around and around in its saucer. "They're so different. So polite. They actually kissed me good night before they went upstairs. It's almost too good to be true."

"But it is true," said her husband.

"I hope so," said Mrs. Gneiss, looking into her cup. She wasn't entirely convinced.

"Stop worrying, Mirjana!" said Mr. Gneiss. "They're fine. Normal. There's nothing wrong with them, nothing! It was just a phase they were going through."

"It was a pretty long phase," Mrs. Gneiss said to her husband. "It lasted eight years."

"But it's over!" He slapped the table for emphasis. "Finished!" He leaned forward. "Do you know what Ned said to me after dinner? He said he wants to learn the business!"

"The restaurant business?"

"The *shish kebab* restaurant business! He said he wants to open up a restaurant just like the Silver Skewer, only profitable." Mr. Gneiss blew his nose. "I have to confess, I was touched."

Mrs. Gneiss sipped her tea. She wanted her husband to be right. But was he? Only time would tell.

chapter 22

"**Y**ou can't take her to school," said Tod on Monday morning. They were on their bikes.

"I'm going to leave her in my locker. She can hear stuff there, and she won't be so lonely." There was no beep from Effie, so Tod knew Tessa was telling the truth.

At first his sister had been overjoyed at Jack's parting gift. She loved Effie, and Jack seemed to know that. When he left on Saturday, he'd given the little e-pet to Tessa for good. "Take care of her," he'd said, and Tessa had burst into tears.

Two days later, Tessa wasn't feeling quite so joyous. She still loved Effie, of course. But she was beginning to understand that owning an e-pet that beeped at lies did present certain problems.

She could never fib to Tod again, for example.

And it was only a matter of time before Lou and Lulu caught on to the reason for Effie's beeping. A totally truthful life! thought Tessa as she pedaled down the dirt road after Tod. Am I up to it?

The minute she got to school she knew she wasn't.

Like sentries, the Gneiss twins stood at the school entrance. They seemed to be waiting for something, and as Tessa and Tod biked up, their heads turned.

Uh-oh, thought Tessa with a shiver of dread. "Tod!" she whispered. "Notso and Never! I think they're waiting for us!"

"So?" Tod's expression, behind the sunglasses Jack had given him, was unfazed. These glasses didn't make him invisible. They just made him look cool.

She shrugged. She could be cool too. If she tried. She followed Tod up the steps.

Ned and Nancy looked a little less neat and perfectly groomed than usual. There was something different about their expressions, too. Holy moly, Tessa thought. They look friendly!

"Hi, Tessa! Hi, Tod!" said the Gneiss twins with blinding smiles. "How *are* you?"

"Okay," mumbled Tod.

"What do you care?" said Tessa.

"We *do* care," said Ned and Nancy. "We care a lot. And we want you to know that we've already talked to Mr. Harken about the whole e-pet thing."

"You have?"

Nancy nodded so vigorously that she looked like a mechanical toy. "We confessed. Told him we took the pets, not you or Mr. Brock."

"Why'd you do it?" Tessa asked.

"To be nice," said Ned and Nancy together.

"No. I mean, why'd you take them in the first place?"

The Gneiss twins looked puzzled. "To tell the truth, we don't remember," said Ned.

"The last few days are just . . . a daze!" said Nancy.

"But we probably took them because they're so cute," said Ned.

"And lovable," said Nancy.

"Whatever," said Tod with disgust. "Now, if you'll excuse me, I have to get to class."

"Wait!" said Ned before he could go. "I've been meaning to ask you—what are you making for the science fair?"

"A wind generator," said Tod, expecting Ned to do or say something creepy. But he didn't. He just stood there, smiling enthusiastically.

"Whoa! That is *so cool*," said Ned. "You really are about the coolest in the school. Isn't he, Nance?"

"Yeah, and with the coolest sister, too," said Nancy, leaning closer to Tessa. "Twins should stick together. That would be megacool, don't you think?"

Tessa backed away as if a snake had slithered over her toes. "Whatever," she said. She managed a little farewell wave and then hurried into school.

Effie would go on the shelf, she decided, opening her locker, right next to her *Black Stallion* figurine. "How come you weren't beeping like crazy?" she whispered to the e-pet. "Weren't they lying?"

But Effie's little face was calm, almost sleepy, not excited the way it got when she was eating lies. Tessa gulped. Once again she pictured Ned and Nancy in the space module. Could it be that their alien abduction had changed them?

Were the Gneiss twins really . . . nice?

That night as they set the table, Tod and Tessa told their grandparents about what had happened. They left out Jack and Jill and the twin planets Gemini. They didn't say anything about Vlad the Impaler. But they did tell Lou and Lulu the latest news about the Gneiss twins.

"All of a sudden they're nice," said Tod.

"Strangely, weirdly nice," said Tessa.

"The change is so radical," said Tod. "It's almost like they mutated or something."

Tessa shot him a warning look. "They even laughed at one of Watson's jokes today," she said. "A really prehistoric one." She imitated Watson's terrible delivery: " 'What do you get when you cross a snowman with a vampire? Frostbite! Yuk, yuk.' "

Tod snorted. So did Lulu. They all sat down.

"People do change," said Lulu. "Sometimes when you least expect it."

"Anyway, it's an improvement," said Lou. "Right?"

The twins made neutral little grunts. They'd talked about Ned and Nancy on the way home from school and come to the conclusion that their transformation might be a hoax.

"They're just too nice," Tessa had said. "I think they're acting." Then she'd had an interesting idea. "Maybe they were changed into aliens—really polite ones, like Jack."

For once Tod hadn't accused her of having an overactive imagination. "Who knows what happened on that module?" he'd said. "Jack promised that their genes would be used to help Gemini, but that doesn't mean they weren't programmed, or given special powers. Maybe they were recruited to some secret intergalactic cause."

"Or maybe they were just changed into harmless aliens—nerdy, superfriendly ones."

Tod had shrugged. "Anything's possible," he'd said. Their father sometimes said this, and for the first time, Tod had seen why. Anything *was* possible.

"We'd better keep our eyes on them," Tessa had finally said. "From a distance."

Now Lou bowed his head for grace. "Thanks for everyone in our family," he said.

"The ones near, the ones far away . . . ," said Lulu, smiling.

"And the ones arriving from Saigon next week," finished Lou with a grin.

"Mom and Dad?"

Lou and Lulu nodded.

"I thought they were coming back in June," said Tessa.

"Their trip went so well they decided to cut it short," said Lou. "They're flying to Paris Wednesday and to New York Sunday."

"They called while you were at school," said Lulu. "They can't wait to see you guys."

"Wow! Great!" said Tessa, but she also kicked

Tod under the table. He looked at her and knew what she was thinking. They loved their parents, but life was about to change. Their parents were a lot less easygoing than Lou and Lulu, and a lot more inquisitive.

"Anyway, thanks for all our blessings," said Lulu.

"And our near and far friends," said Tod, thinking of Jack and Jill, wherever they might be.

"Especially the newest ones," said Tessa, "the Gneiss twins!"

Beep BEEP! said Effie.

"What was that about?" asked Lulu as she passed the carrots.

"Just making sure everybody gets fed," said Tessa.

ABOUT THE AUTHORS

Stephanie Spinner is the coauthor with Jonathan Etra of *Aliens for Breakfast*, which won the Texas Bluebonnet Award, and its companions, *Aliens for Lunch* and *Aliens for Dinner*. She lives in New York City.

Terry Bisson's *Bears Discover Fire* won both the Hugo and the Nebula Award, science fiction's highest honors. His *Pirates of the Universe* was a *New York Times* Notable Book of 1996. He too lives in New York City.